HOLD ON TIGHT

Heather Klassen

Unionville, NY

For Sennen and Tress, of course

Cover art by Milton Kemnitz

Royal Fireworks Press
First Avenue, PO Box 399
Unionville, NY 10988-0399
(845) 726-4444
FAX: (845) 726-3824
email: mail@rfwp.com
website: rfwp.com

ISBN: 978-0-88092-716-1

Printed and bound in the United States of America using vegetable-based inks on acid-free, recycled paper and environmentally-friendly cover coatings by the Royal Fireworks Printing Co. of Unionville, New York.

CHAPTER 1

Draft

My days were summer-plaid and popsicle-purple until Bobby had to go.

My days were tree-climbed and skinned-knee red until my brother left.

A week into summer, I perched in the crook of the apple tree, flicking the wormy green apples from their skimpy hold on the knotted grayed-bark branches. Soft thuds when the fruit hit the ground. Drips of grape on my thigh, melted popsicle leaving sticky streams on my skin.

A slamming car door made me look up, past the brick of the house, to the driveway. My father, home in the middle of a workday.

I slid down from the tree, popsicle stick clenched between my teeth, my tongue trying to escape the cottony-wood taste. I scraped my knee against the bark, opened another scab, exposing bright red blood.

I ran across the yard, bristly dry grass scraping my heels. Then my bare feet felt the cool concrete patio. June, not hot enough yet to scorch the bottoms of feet. I yanked on the metal handle, sending the glass door sliding along its track, and slipped inside.

My parents stood in the kitchen, my mother leaning back against the sink, her sleeveless housedress wrinkled in front as if a child had just sat in her lap, wrinkling the material by fidgeting and squirming. But Bobby and I had been too old for laps for a long time. Bobby much longer than me.

My father stood next to the kitchen table, one hand gripping the back of a chair. The chair where Bobby always sat. My father's white shirt was rumpled already, just past noon. But his short black hair, slicked into place, looked the same as when he had left that morning, the same as all day, every day.

I slipped the damp popsicle stick into the pocket of my shorts, and waited. I didn't lean back against the glass door, not wanting to leave handprints for my mother to clean. I wanted to hear what they said, everything. I wanted to know. But the Rolling Stones pounded out of Bobby's room, the beat vibrating the walls and our ears, and I didn't know if I would hear, could hear.

As Mick's voice faded out, before the next song began, my father spoke.

"He needs to go, Marna," my father said. "He's eighteen. When I was his age, I did my part. And I came back just fine. That war made me the man I am today."

"But we could go, take Bobby…" my mother paused, watching my father's frown deepen, "to Canada." My mother said the word that had been a presence in my house for months, but like a prized jewel encased in a glass museum display, none of us could quite grasp onto it. But we knew it existed, within reach. If only.

My father shook his head, and the Rolling Stones stopped, as if his shaking head had lifted the needle from the record. My parents waited, spoke no more words, because they knew that the end of the music signaled Bobby's appearance.

The three of us watched my brother as he stepped into the kitchen, his bare feet mirroring mine, but larger, darker. Bobby always tanned more quickly than me. He looked first at my father, who glanced away. My father couldn't stand Bobby's hair that summer, flat dark hair that hung to his shoulders. I didn't know if that's why my father looked away then, so he didn't have to see the hair. Maybe because of something else.

"Bobby." My mother stepped away from the sink, reached out, touched my brother's arm. It seemed that my mother and

Bobby could never be in the same room without my mother touching him. The same way she would squeeze my shoulder or rub my arm, the same way she loved us without saying it out loud. My mother touched Bobby, even though my father complained, saying, "Marna, he's a man now, when will you stop all this lovey-dovey mama's boy stuff with him?"

My mother never answered that question. But I knew the answer, knew it as if the word had been tattooed across my mother's right arm, the one that touched us most often. The answer was *never*.

"We could still go, Bobby," my mother said, lifting her free hand to her hair, patting the curlered-in waves, her nervous gesture. "We could go to Canada, just say it, and I'll take you there. Just agree to it, Bobby, and we, Suzanne and I, we'll stay with you. Forever, if we have to."

"Stop it with this Canada business," my father said, not giving Bobby a chance to answer my mother. "You know that's foolishness, Marna; stop filling his head with your foolishness. He's a man now, and he'll do what he needs to do."

"I'll be okay, Mom," my brother said, pulling his arm away from her fingertips, her touch. "It's only for a year. That's nothing. I'll be back before you know it, and then maybe I'll quit working at the garage and find a decent job, like Dad's always on my case about. Maybe I'll even start those classes over at the junior college."

My mother listened, tried to smile at Bobby's plans, couldn't.

"Hey, maybe this time away will be good for me," Bobby continued. "Maybe it'll help me grow up like Dad's always saying I need to. Make a man out of me." Bobby looked at my father and grinned, his joker grin.

My father shook his head, shaking off Bobby's sarcasm. "Look, Bobby, I have to make up this time at work. Are you ready or not?"

3

"I have to get my shoes. I wasn't sure you were here yet. Give me a minute." Bobby turned and left, and I crossed the kitchen floor and followed him, trailing the back of his denim shorts and black tee shirt down the hall.

In his room, Bobby jammed his feet into the unlaced sneakers half kicked beneath his bed, and turned around.

He smiled as he saw me standing in the doorway.

"Hey, silent Suzanne, what are you staring at?" he asked.

"Mom doesn't want you to go," I said.

Bobby shrugged, his hated hair brushing across his shoulders.

"When your number's up, it's up," my brother told me. "I don't really see a choice. The Canada thing is just Mom's wild imagination. Besides, if we don't stop the communists from taking over the world, who will? We're Americans, that's our job," Bobby echoed our father's dinner table lectures. "But hey, Suze, Mom shouldn't worry so much. I'll be back. But probably without my hair. I hear they really do a job on it. Dad will like that, don't you think?"

I nodded, knowing the answer to that question. The one about the communists, I had no idea. "Sure," I agreed.

Bobby took a step toward me, saw I didn't move, and stopped.

"I don't want you to go either," I said.

Bobby put both hands behind his head, gripped his hair into a ponytail, then let it fall. His nervous habit, my mother called it. Like her hair habit, though she never connected the two. She couldn't see her own hands, her own hair. Only Bobby's.

"Suzy-Q, right now I'm just going down to sign some papers or something. Get official, I don't know, this is more Dad's trip than mine. I won't be *leaving* leaving for a few more days." Bobby watched me with his dark brown eyes, chocolate syrup eyes, I always thought. "I'm not abandoning my little sister

4

yet. And I keep telling you, I'll be back in not much more than a year. You'll be what, twelve?"

I nodded. Yes, twelve and a half next spring. A lifetime away from eleven and a half, to me. A summer and a fall and a winter and a spring, all with Bobby gone.

"When I get back, we'll finish that engine on the Chevy, okay?"

I nodded again. "Okay."

"Wouldn't that be something, to get that old heap up and running?" my brother asked. "No more parts scattered across the driveway for Dad to gripe about."

"Yeah," I agreed, "that'd be something."

"And you, Suzy-Q, get first ride. But look, I really have to go now. Dad will have an attack if I'm not out there soon."

And Bobby walked past me, out of the room, but not before he gave my shoulder a squeeze, one of my mother's I-love-you squeezes, but with my brother's large, grease-stained hand. A car mechanic's hand. *Not a soldier's hand,* I thought. But then, I didn't really know. I never knew a soldier before.

I heard the front door open and close, and my father's car starting up in the driveway, and I sat down on Bobby's bed, on the unmade sheets and crumpled comforter, and I looked from one poster tacked onto the wall to the next. Hendrix, Jagger, Dylan, I could name them all. Bobby talked, all the time, talked about the music, the meaning of the lyrics. But me, I just listened to those songs because Bobby let me hang out with him, invited me into his room to listen, to share his music with him.

The floor in the hallway creaked and I looked up to see my mother taking my place in the doorway.

"He's still here for a few more days," I said.

"I know," my mother said.

"He'll be back, Mom, really he will," I told her.

"I know," she agreed. "I know you want that as much as I do, Suzanne. So we'll want it together, okay?"

Then my mother tried to smile at me, and I tried to smile back. It was hard. I think Bobby meant the same to us, my mother and me. Sometimes I thought she didn't really see me; she was only seeing Bobby. At least for the last few months, ever since he turned eighteen, ever since the draft became what we talked about at dinner almost every night. But I didn't mind. Wanting Bobby to come back would be something my mother and I could do together, just like loving him was what we did together now.

After my mother tried to smile at me, but couldn't, she moved on down the hallway, toward her room, and I sat on Bobby's bed knowing he'd be back. My brother always did what he said he would.

So I knew he'd come back from Vietnam. In one year. And I'd be twelve then, and he'd get the Chevy running and take me for the first ride, to the Tastee-Freeze. And treat me to a cone, a chocolate-vanilla swirl. And together we'd lick the drips from our cones before they dropped sticky, onto our summer clothes, licking along with Jimi Hendrix's guitar licks on the radio that Bobby always had to have playing, anytime he drove or rode in a car. So I knew we'd be listening, even with the car stopped, sitting in Bobby's Chevy parked in the gravel lot in front of the Tastee-Freeze.

I smiled, thinking about Bobby coming back and how it would be, and I could almost taste those two flavors, creamy chocolate and sweet vanilla, melting together on my tongue.

CHAPTER 2

Movies

And then my brother left, and we drove back from the airport, my father dropping my mother and me off in the driveway on his way back to work. My mother went into her bedroom, shut the door, probably still wiping her eyes like she did at the airport, probably still silent like she was the whole way home. She didn't answer my father when he spoke to her, didn't respond when he told her not to act like this. My mother would act how she felt, I knew.

For days my mother spent a lot of time in her bedroom, coming out to make meals and move the clothes from the washer to the dryer. We didn't talk much. I watched TV, let the cartoons and game shows wash over me, and I read my book club books over again, and one day I sat on the nubby sofa in the living room, my fingers tracing Vietnam on the usually ignored globe on the end table. The tracing didn't take much time. Long and skinny, Vietnam didn't seem like much of a country.

Bobby in Vietnam. Was he there yet? I didn't know. I knew that he had to go somewhere else first, learn how to be a soldier. Learn about weapons and maybe marching, I didn't know what else.

"Vietnam." I tried the word out on my tongue. I don't think I had ever said it out loud before, though I had been hearing that word for months, for years. First just on the TV news. Then in my house, spoken by my family, mostly by my father, not so much my mother and brother.

I covered the country with the tip of my finger. Bobby in Vietnam. I tried to imagine how he could fit his loud wild self into that skinny land. His Mick Jagger imitations, thrusting his lips out, pillow-like, prancing around his bedroom, shouting along with the words, *can't get no satisfaction*, into an imaginary microphone.

Would he have music there? I didn't know. A year without his music, his records spinning endlessly on the turntable, only quick breaks to lift the needle, put another record on, I couldn't imagine that for Bobby.

And then I felt Canada, traced its borders with my fingertips. A big country, close to home, big enough for Bobby, all of Bobby. And his loud music and his wild prancing. But he didn't want to go there. Or couldn't. I didn't know which.

All I knew was that he didn't go to Canada. Instead, he went to Vietnam, to do his part. That's what my father kept saying. Over and over. Bobby's part. He's doing his part. *What is his part?* I wondered. I didn't know what anybody's part in this war could be.

I didn't want to listen last year in school, when Mrs. Richards talked about Vietnam. Social Studies is boring. I didn't listen when she explained who was fighting whom and why. I thought it had nothing to do with me. Only soldiers, and I knew no soldiers.

I didn't listen to the kids in my class, the ones who claimed that our country had to go and fight there, the one or two others who said that their parents felt the war was wrong, maybe our country shouldn't be there. Well, I listened some. But not much.

The dinner conversations at my house changed from what did you do in school today and the sale on towels at Kaufman's to the war and draft notices. It was then that I started listening at home, and wished that I had listened at school.

But I guess my listening wouldn't have made any difference anyway. Or my mother and me telling Bobby that we didn't want him to go. He went anyway.

I slapped the globe with the palm of my hand, sent it spinning, the countries all melting together into a blurry colorful mass.

I stood up, walked through the kitchen and into the family room where my mother sat on the older, worn sofa, out of her room, folding towels. She stared at the TV, at the characters on *Guiding Light* as they moved from offices to houses to hospital waiting rooms, always talking, their whole lives talking. But my mother watched with the sound off, so the actors looked strange with their mouths moving and moving but nothing coming out. Silent, like me sometimes, like my brother teased me when I preferred thinking to talking. My mother used to watch TV with the volume up but didn't anymore, not since Bobby left.

My mother, halfway through a towel, looked up at me. "Suzanne, you should call Kathy back and go to that movie."

I shook my head.

"You need to see your friends; you need to have fun." My mother paused in her towel folding. "Life goes on, Suzanne. We can't spend the next year just waiting."

Who are you kidding, Mom? I wanted to say. My mother, who jumped every time the phone rang, grabbing it before the first ring even ended. Mom, who pretended not to be waiting for the mailman, but just happened to be looking out the front door each afternoon as he lugged his bag to our mailbox.

But if she could pretend, so could I. I could pretend to have fun. Pretend a normal summer day. If it would make my mother feel better. If it would make her think that at least one of her children was fine, just fine. I wanted my mother to be happy. I knew she wanted me to be happy. So I would pretend for her. "Okay, Mom," I agreed. "I'll call Kathy."

The arrangements made, I sat on the front steps, five dollars in my pocket, my mother saying I should get popcorn too as she pulled the bill from her purse. I waited for Kathy and her mother to drive up, take me to the movie, take me to have fun.

Finally their dirt-colored Plymouth pulled into the driveway, onto my father's side, Bobby's Chevy filling the other space, and I stood up, smoothing down the front of my culottes. Wear something a little nicer, my mother had said, than those raggedy shorts. So we compromised on the culottes, shorts pretending to be a skirt, the five dollars tucked into the plaid pocket.

I climbed into the car, into the back seat next to Kathy. Kathy wore culottes too and flat white sandals like the ones my mother bought me but I refused to wear.

"Suzanne, I haven't even seen you since the last day of school," Kathy said. "What have you been doing?"

I shrugged. "Oh, stuff."

Mrs. Wilson turned around to smile at me. "I heard that your brother enlisted, Suzanne."

Drafted, I thought, but didn't correct her.

"Yes," I replied. "He left last Tuesday."

"You must be so proud of him," Mrs. Wilson said, her smile never changing as she spoke.

"I wish I had a big brother who could go fight in the war," Kathy said. "I'd be so proud of him."

I didn't look at Kathy. Instead, I pretended to study the American flag decal stuck in the corner of the car window next to me. I picked at the edge of it with my fingernail. I tried to think about being proud. *The Wilsons must be proud about the war*, I thought. *That's what this flag means. If Kathy had a brother in the war, they'd be proud of him for going, for becoming a soldier. It's easy to think that*, I thought, *when it isn't real for you.*

Like it is for my family. Is my father proud of Bobby? I wondered. He wanted Bobby to go; he thought that it was right, but I didn't remember him ever talking about pride. Not around

Bobby, at least. What I remembered most from the months before Bobby left was my father yelling about the hair, his yelling "Why do you want to look like a girl, why, Bobby, why?" As if hair were the most important issue in the time that Bobby had left at home, as if changing his hair would change anything.

Well, when Bobby comes home, he won't have that hair, that's what he told me. So Dad can quit yelling about that, maybe start talking about pride, instead.

Kathy's mother let us out in front of the theater, promising to pick us up in two hours when the movie got out. As Kathy and I walked up and joined the line, we saw two boys we knew from school standing several people in front of us.

Ricky, one of the boys from our class last year, called, "Why don't you cut?"

Kathy blushed, her freckles brightening against the pink of her skin. I knew she liked Ricky, her fifth-grade crush, but she shook her head. She wouldn't break the rules by cutting in line; didn't want to make the people in front of us angry.

So Ricky and his friend Kevin left their group and walked back to us, and I thought they wanted to talk to Kathy, but no, they stopped next to me. They wanted to talk to me.

But they wanted to talk about Bobby. Not about me.

"My sister said your brother just went to Vietnam, Suzanne," Kevin told me, running his hand over his bristly crew cut hair.

I nodded, but didn't know what to say, didn't know what he wanted me to tell him. *Yes, Bobby left. What else could I say?*

"They get to use the coolest guns," Ricky said, jamming his hands into the pockets of his army green shorts. "Your brother is so lucky, Suzanne. He gets to fight for us, kill those gooks."

Gooks? I looked at Ricky, not sure what he was saying. Bobby had never said anything like that. He only talked about communists and only once in a while.

"Aren't you proud of him?" Kevin asked me.

11

"Sure," I answered. Because I did feel proud of my brother. Not because he went to the war, but because of the person he had always been. My older brother. But now it seemed that everyone, adults and kids my age, wanted me to feel proud because my brother had become a soldier, and it was hard to not let that feeling seep into me. Now I had something that none of my friends did: a brother who went to the war. Now I would be singled out, paid attention to. It was hard not to let that feel good. In a way.

As the line began to move, Ricky and Kevin backed away from us, saying "See you inside" and "Why don't you sit near us?" and rejoined their friends. Kathy, blushing, and I, fingering my five dollar bill, were swept into the freezer-cold theater with the crowd, through the popcorn line, and into our seats. We didn't sit with Kevin and Ricky, but two rows behind them, off to the side. That way Kathy could see Ricky, watch him during the movie, but not be too close, not have to think of things to say to him.

The plush seats felt smooth on the backs of my thighs; the air conditioning felt cool on my bare arms and face. I listened to Kathy chattering on about Ricky, "Isn't he cute, isn't he nice?" until the lights dimmed, went out, and the movie began in the darkened theater. Then I munched on popcorn and watched the movie, and even laughed at the funny parts, laughed at the parts where Herbie the Love Bug, who was really a car, a Volkswagon Beetle—but you almost thought he was human, the way he acted—won the races and made the other race car drivers mad.

At the end, back outside, blinking at the sunlight hurting my movie-theater eyes, I still laughed, Kathy and I retelling the scenes to each other. And then the Plymouth pulled up, we slid into our seats and headed home.

As we drove and Kathy relayed the plot of the movie to her barely listening mother, I realized, when I saw that flag decal again, that I had hardly thought of Bobby, or not at all, for the past two hours, not since the movie started. And that actually felt good. I felt eleven and happy, like my friends, enjoying a Disney movie and buttered popcorn on a summer day.

Mom's right, I thought, *life does go on. Bobby's in Vietnam, but he'll be okay, and we'll be here and okay,* and I couldn't wait to get home to tell my mother that I understood. About life going on and needing to have fun. Not even pretending it, doing it for real.

And so after I shut the door on the Plymouth, I hurried up the front walk and into the house, calling, "Mom? Mom?"

I didn't find her in the living room or kitchen or family room or her bedroom or mine or Bobby's. She wouldn't go anywhere without leaving me a note, and besides, we didn't have a second car. I mean, besides Bobby's Chevy in the driveway, and that didn't work anyway. So I knew she had to be downstairs, in the basement. Laundry day, like every day this summer, it seemed.

I opened the door to the basement, but faced only dark, dark except for a flicker of light against one wall. I crouched down to see, to figure out what the flicker could be, and I realized that my mother wasn't doing laundry. I saw from the flicker's glow that she reclined back in one of our beanbag chairs and she stared toward the wall, at the movie screen she had set up.

My mother had been watching movies too, but not movie theater movies, home movies. Movies of me and Bobby.

I started down the stairs. We hadn't watched those movies for a long time. Now I wanted to watch them too.

CHAPTER 3

A Letter

The movies I found my mother watching started with me as a toddler in sleeveless sunsuits, Bobby as an eight-year-old wearing shorts and shirts in tones of black, white, and gray, because back then, home movies could only be made in black and white. When I was little, that's when they bought the movie camera, the screen, the projector. That's when they started taking movies of us. Before that, they only had a regular camera, so the first seven years of Bobby's life, and my infancy, could only be traced by looking at those small squares of posed people glued into the photo albums tucked into a drawer in my mother's room.

When they bought the movie camera, my parents couldn't stop making movies. Of me. Of Bobby. Of me and Bobby together, every birthday party, every Christmas, every summer trip to the beach. My father had the camera in his hands everywhere we went, it seemed. My father, so proud of his kids, at least back then, was rarely in the movies, almost always behind the camera, calling instructions to us. Bobby, do this. Suzanne, show us that. My mother flitted in and out of the scenes, helping with this, fixing that. They filmed everything, every event, until Bobby became a teenager and started objecting, but then we hardly ever watched the movies, anyway. Too much work to set up the projector and the screen and to load the reels and rewind, over and over. I didn't remember the last time they took a movie of me, not in the last year, I knew.

I crossed the basement, dragging the other bean bag chair across the floor with me. When I reached the place where my mother sat, I stopped next to her and sank into the blue vinyl, the chair molding itself around me.

On the screen, I toddled across the backyard grass, wearing a flowered sunsuit and little wisps of hair, toward Bobby's eight-year-old outstretched arms.

Home movies were silent, not like theater movies, and so it didn't matter if you talked. No lines to miss, no audience to annoy.

"He was crazy about you when you were little, Suzanne," my mother spoke first. "I was so happy to have my little girl finally, and Bobby, he was so happy to have a little sister. It surprised us, it really did, the way he took to you. Most little boys don't care about babies at all."

I didn't say anything. Just watched us, me and Bobby.

"He used to push you up and down the driveway in your stroller, for an hour if I needed him to, so I could get some work done. Sometimes he'd run, pushing you too fast, pretending to be a race car, I guess, but you loved it. I'd look out the window and see your little arms waving, a big grin on your face," my mother told me. "He wanted to help with you. He really didn't mind at all. He never complained, oh maybe a couple of times he did, about missing something with his buddies because of you."

The scene on the screen changed to a birthday, party hats and streamers, and a two-year-old me, grabbing for the candles on my cake, Bobby's hands closing over mine, so I couldn't touch the flames.

"You were too far apart to really play together much," my mother said. "But I remember Bobby patiently playing tea party with you, pretending to drink tea from those little china cups."

My mother looked away from the screen, at me. "Do you remember that tea set, Suzanne? Whatever happened to that?"

"It broke," I said, remembering that day, dropping the shoebox, watching the lid pop off, the broken china pieces scattering across the floor. And trying to pick every small sharp shard up from the carpet before my mother discovered the mess. And then walking on the little prickly left behind pieces until the next time my mother vacuumed. "I do remember Bobby playing tea party with me, but he would've been really angry with me if I ever told his friends about it."

My mother smiled; I could see the smile lit by the faint glow of the screen, which she watched again.

"He never let any of his friends tease you," my mother said. "He was always a good big brother."

"Is," I told her. I didn't remind her that sometimes Bobby got mad at me, sometimes he teased me or even yelled at me, like that time last year when I scratched one of his records, by accident. He yelled at me, "Why do you have to be so clumsy sometimes, Suzanne, why?" But then he knew it had been an accident and "Okay," he said, "just pay me back and we'll forget about it," and I did pay him back, and he never mentioned it again.

He could get mad at me; sometimes I even got mad at him, but it never lasted. It couldn't between Bobby and me.

My mother turned to look at me again, stared at me for at least a minute before speaking. "Yes, *is*," she agreed.

I watched the movies with her, through a Christmas, Bobby helping me to unwrap doll furniture, Playdoh sets, and a green Gumby and orange Pokey, Bobby showing me his new racetrack, his Hot Wheels cars, silently mouthing the words, "You can watch me race them, Suzanne, but don't touch. Not until you're older."

When I did get older, Bobby did let me play with that racetrack. I remember the little metal cars zipping down the plastic track, through the loop, and then to the finish line. By that time, Bobby had grown almost too old for the cars and the track, instead talking all the time about buying an electric guitar and an amp, and wanting me to listen to the new 45 he just bought. "Listen to this, Suzanne, just listen to it," he'd say as the record dropped onto the turntable. And I listened to every song, liked them because he did.

Finally, one day he just gave me the racetrack and the cars, and I kneeled on the carpet in my room, running races while Bobby, in his room across the hall, picked out chords on the guitar he bought with car washing and snow shoveling money. From then on, Bobby's own music added to the music pounding through our house, sometimes too late, past my bedtime, and then my father would yell, "Knock it off Bobby, Suzanne needs to sleep." My father never knew that I could almost sleep better feeling the beat of Bobby's bass vibrating through the skin on my chest.

The movie faded out on a scene of Bobby pulling me on a wooden sled, me making it harder by dragging my mittened hands through the snow. I didn't mean to make it harder for him. I just didn't know. I was just a little kid then.

My mother stood up and reached for the projector, to stop the reel, to stop the click click click of the end of the film whirling around and around. She took the reel off.

"I need to do laundry," she said, but she reached into the box for another movie, another chapter of her children's lives.

And then I didn't want to sit there in that dark basement anymore, watching my brother and me and our lives flicker across that screen, mouthing silent shouts at found Easter eggs. My mother said that life had to go on, and I tried with mine, I went to the movie, I had fun, I went on, but she sat in the basement, only going backward.

Why won't she do anything with me? I wondered. We used to spend hours together sometimes, all the craft stuff spread out on the kitchen table, stringing beads, or baking, my mom loved to bake cookies and always let me help. Or in the summer, like now, we'd go on walks, and sometimes she'd even ride Bobby's outgrown bike, and I'd ride mine, all the way to the park. She would even get silly, like a kid, almost, and we'd ride double down the slide and push each other on the swings. But now I think if I asked her to do something with me, she'd say she had to do laundry. Or something else. But never anything with me.

"I'm going outside," I said, standing up.

"Okay," my mother replied. "It's summertime. You should play outside, Suzanne. Get some sun."

"Kathy wants me to go to the pool with her sometime next week," I said.

"The pool? Good," my mother replied. She stopped fiddling with the reel in her hand and looked over the projector at me. I could see my mother's face in the dim light from the screen. She smiled at me, almost the way she used to smile before. Before Bobby left. "Swimming is fun. That will be good for you, Suzanne."

I nodded, then went up the stairs, into the light of the kitchen and then outside, into the backyard. I headed for my blanket tent, the one I built the day before, stretched out between two trees, the one my mother said I could leave up until it started to rain.

I checked the clothespins, their grip still firm on the clothesline and the blankets, and then I slipped inside, crawled onto the old sheet, thin with washing, that my mother let me use.

Inside my blanket tent the air felt warmer than outside, the sun heating the cloth walls. A faint scent of detergent and cut grass drifted through when the breeze rustled the blankets. Sometimes I brought a book into my tents to read; sometimes I just sat and thought. Sometimes I chased bugs back outside and sometimes I let them stay so I could try to change their route by nudging them with a blade of grass.

I never invited anyone into my tents, but once in a while a kid from the neighborhood would poke his head in while I sat inside, then quickly pull himself back out and run away. I knew that sometimes kids played in my tents when I was gone. They left their evidence, empty Pixie Stix wrappers and crumpled up sheet corners. I liked the sheet smoothed out flat on the grass beneath.

That day I sat in my tent and thought about my mother sitting in the dark basement watching home movies. She never used to do that, at least not by herself, not on a hot summer day. Last summer she even crawled into my tent with me a few times. She didn't have to be invited; she was my mother. She said she liked my tents, the summer smells, the hiding away with me, just with me. But this summer, she didn't visit me in my tents. Not even once. How long would she sit in the dark basement? All day? Every day?

No, not all day. After a while, as I lay on my back, watching a sliver of sky through a gap in my tent, I heard my mother calling me from the back door.

"Suzanne," she called, hard on the -anne. "Could you go get the mail please? I saw the mailman, but I'm in the middle of making meatloaf."

I poked my head out of my blanket tent. Had to squeeze out onto the grass, trying to not disturb the clothespins. They came unclipped easily. Then the tent sides would collapse, burying me in hot summer blankets. Tangled up, unable to breathe.

I walked around the side of the house, my feet feeling the scratchiness of the drying rain-starved grass, and then on to the driveway. My bare feet danced across the broiling black tar. I reached the mailbox and yanked the little metal door open. Reached in, pulled out the mail.

White envelopes that looked like the bills my father always groaned about. A magazine promising ten recipes for summer appetites. A flimsy piece of cardboard, an ad for a summer furniture clearance. And then another white envelope, but not a neatly typed address across the front, instead an inked scrawl. Bobby's scrawl.

"Mom!" I yelled, racing across the driveway and up the front steps. "Mom!" I called, holding the envelope up in front of me, the other mail, the forgotten mail, gripped in my other hand. "A letter! From Bobby!"

The first one. My mother met me at the door, little bits of ground meat still clinging to her fingers. She tore into the envelope, pulled out folded notebook paper. Tucked inside hers, she found a smaller folded up note. For me.

My mother sank down onto the floor and read her letter. At first I watched my mother reading. The letter shook in her hand. My mother's eyes weren't crying, but her smile seemed pretend. An achy make-believe kind of smile. I watched my mother for a minute or two.

Then I opened my letter from Bobby.

CHAPTER 4

In Country

"Hey Suzy-Q," my brother wrote. "This is one weird trip. One of the first things they gave us at training camp were dog tags. To wear around our necks, with our names and other info on them. Makes me think they can't tell the difference between humans and animals. Funny, huh?"

Yeah, funny, I thought, tracing the words that Bobby wrote to me with my fingertips.

Hard to picture Bobby as a dog. I smiled.

"Tell Dad that the hair is no more. They clipped it all off and shaved the sides, too. All the guys had to watch their hair go. Man, I never saw so much hair on any floor before. Guess I wasn't the only one trying to look like a girl, as Dad would say. Ha ha."

I could almost see Bobby through his words. Same goofy smile, same squinty, glinty eyes. Less hair, though. Maybe now he looked like the Bobby in the home movies my mother and I watched, the nine- and ten-year-old Bobby with short, bristly hair.

"Another weird thing, Suze, is the guns. Now I got me one, and what a strange trip that is. I never have held a gun before, not a real one, just that BB gun Rob got for Christmas when we were twelve, but his dad took it away because he kept shooting birds, not cans like he was supposed to. He let me shoot it a couple of times before it got taken away. I never wanted one for myself, though. I don't know, it felt weird, not my kind of thing, I guess.

"I made some buddies at training camp, but when we all shipped out (okay, really we went in airplanes but they don't say you flew out) to Nam we got split up and put in different companies. I'm not allowed to tell you what mine's called, or where I'm at even, but kiddo, that's okay, I figure you were never much for geography anyway."

The word geography makes me remember the spinning, spinning globe, the colorful whirl and how it made me feel like we all have to hold on tight to where we are or if we let go, even for a second, we might go spinning off of the world. *Hold on tight, Bobby*, I thought. *Hold on to the other side of the world. And I'll hold on to my side just as tight.*

"So anyway now I got to make me some new buddies and then just see what happens next. I'm writing to you before they really send me in country, that's what they call being in the war in Vietnam, except they call it Nam here. I hope I get to go with some of my new buddies, or else I'll have to start all over again. With making friends, I mean.

"Suzy-Q, you have a fun summer. Go swimming with your friends, do stuff like that. Stay away from the boys, like I told you before. Sorry I acted like a jerk when that little runt called you that time, but it's my job to protect my little sister, right? Now I'm not around to do that, so just don't answer the phone, okay, Suze? Okay, just kidding, but I don't want us staying mad at each other over something as dumb as boys. And I do mean dumb. Anyway, keep telling Mom that I'll be okay, because I will, I'm smart enough to keep out of trouble, but Mom, the way she is, she still thinks I'm two or something and need to hold her hand to cross the street.

"Gotta go now, they're after us about something we have to do, maybe go fight the communists and beat them so we can go home. I'll write whenever I can, Suze. So long."

I looked up from the letter and at my mom and she looked up from hers, second time through.

"He's okay, Mom," I said. "Just like he said he would be." And still thinking I'm mad at him for acting like a jerk that one time, but I'm not. He should know that. Scratched records and phone calls from boys, not important stuff. Not between me and Bobby.

"I know," my mother replied. She folded her letter, slipped it into the envelope. She looked at her hands, at the little flecks of meat dotting her skin. "Now I have to go finish that meatloaf so I'll have dinner on the table when your father gets home."

And she stood up, tried to smooth out the wrinkles on her yellow and orange striped dress, and headed for the kitchen. Where I knew she'd finish preparing the meatloaf and the beans and the rolls and when everything was either in the oven or simmering on the stove, she'd mark off one more day on the calendar.

One more day of waiting for Bobby to come home.

CHAPTER 5

Midnight Monopoly

My mother pulled into the parking lot of the A&P, guided our station wagon in between two painted lines. Saturday, grocery shopping day. My mother had the car while my father cut the grass. Parched grass, not much to cut, but he liked to keep it all even, all trimmed. Just like the neighbors did.

As we crossed the parking lot, passing the rows of cars, I noticed that there were more people hanging around in front of the store than usual. More than just the regular Saturday shoppers, the young mothers in to-the-knee shorts, trying to drag little boys in cowboy hats away from the mechanical horse ride in front. "Please, Mommy, just one more ride, just one more ride," their voices called above the rattle of pushed shopping carts—regular Saturday sounds to me.

My mother and I walked past the people, these extra people, and I didn't look at them, instead I looked down and watched my Keds—holes where my big toenails always poked through the canvas after a couple months of wearing them—cross the end of the asphalt parking lot, and then the sidewalk, then across the rubber mat and into the store. A feeling clung to me as the grocery store air conditioning slapped my skin, a feeling that something different would happen that day. A sunny shopping Saturday. A day when unusual people milled around outside the store where my mother and I bought our groceries every Saturday morning.

I pushed the cart through the store, stopping where my mother stopped, waiting while she compared the prices on boxes of tea bags, waiting while she pulled a crumpled list from her vinyl pocketbook to consult as we cruised the aisles.

"Which kind?" my mother asked as we stood in front of the freezer section, staring down at box after box of ice cream, nestled together in straight rows. "Your favorite?"

"Chocolate chip mint," I agreed, knowing that my mother still tried to please me, just like I tried to please her, even this summer when everything seemed hard to us. But I could help by setting the table, folding the laundry, pulling a smile from her, and she tried to make me happy with ice cream, my favorite kind. I watched as my mother scooped up one hard rectangular box of frozen ice cream. She dropped it into the cart on top of our other groceries and steered me and the cart toward the checkout line.

We had too many bags to carry, so I pushed the cart through the doors that opened all by themselves, magic doors, at least that's what my mother called them when they installed them at the A&P. Bobby and I used to race each other to see which one of us would be the one to start the magic that day, even when he got too old to care, like twelve, but he still liked to race because I did. To me, at six, the magic still felt new and worth racing for.

Outside, my mother and I had to stop, our way blocked by the extra people, and then I understood what those extra people had been doing. Getting ready. Getting their signs ready.

The extra people, the non-shoppers, stood in front of us, lined up along the sidewalk, blocking our way to the parking lot and our car. We waited. I couldn't push the cart through the people.

"Mom?" I questioned, thinking maybe she would know what to do, would have the answer, the way mothers are supposed to. But she looked at me as if she thought that I might have the answer, and she gripped the side of the cart as if she had to hold on tight.

I knew who these people were now. *Protestors.* I had seen people like them on TV, on the news. Holding their signs.

Chanting their words. I knew these people existed, but I never thought I'd see any at the A&P. I thought they would stay on TV where they belonged.

I looked at the protestors as they chanted. The men had more hair even than Bobby did, before, at least. The women wore their hair long, to their butts, past the pockets of their jeans. The jeans were ripped or patched or both. The men wore headbands to hold their hair back, dark sunglasses shielding their eyes. *They all look alike*, I thought.

They held signs. I read them. "Stop the Killing," I read. And, "Get Out of Vietnam."

My mother finally found her voice. "Please let us through," she said. "We just want to go home."

"So do the soldiers, lady," a man called to my mother, a break in his chanting.

"Please," my mother said. "My son is there."

"How could you let him go?" One of the women, a girl really, I guess, a teenager with long flat hair and jeans, wide at the bottom, yelled at my mother. "How could you?"

"It wasn't a matter of letting," my mother said, her voice flat like that girl's hair. She let go of the cart, shifted her pocketbook from one arm to the other, lifted her free hand to my shoulder, squeezed my shoulder, to reassure me or herself, I didn't know. "Please let us through. Our ice cream is melting."

"Oh, your ice cream is melting." A woman stepped closer to us, a woman my mother's age, but not dressed like my mother, no freshly pressed dress, no pocketbook, no lipstick. She wore jeans like the others, clunky sandals, her hair long and loose, not put up in curlers the night before, I could tell. She stood in front of my mother, clutching the wooden handle of her sign. "Well, our sons are dying."

Her words stung me like a hard slap. *No*, I wanted to say, *no, your sons will come home, just like Bobby. Don't worry, it'll be okay.* But I didn't say that. Somehow I knew my words wouldn't help.

The magic doors behind us slid open, and a man stepped out of the store, walked up to stand next to my mother and me. I could tell from his blazer with the logo that he worked in the store, saw his tie and thought he could be the manager.

"You all get out of here!" he yelled at the protestors. "This is private property. I've called the police!"

The group, the protestors, turned their attention to him, away from us. My mother grabbed the side of the cart again, and I pushed through a gap in the protestors, and we crossed the parking lot to our station wagon, hurrying, almost hitting the brown paneled sides of the car with the shopping cart when we stopped.

My mother swung open the door on the back of the car and together we shoved the bags inside. I grabbed the empty cart, turned back toward the store.

"Leave it, Suzanne," my mother said, as she unlocked her car door.

Leave the cart? My father would have a fit if I left the cart in the parking lot, start talking about dings in car doors and do you know how much they cost to repair, but I left the cart right there in the middle of the parking lot because my mother told me to.

I slid into the front seat next to my mother, and I waited for her to start the car, but she didn't, and I looked over and saw how her hands trembled as she clutched the steering wheel. *Mom, what are you afraid of?* I wanted to ask. *Why didn't you yell back at those people? Why didn't you tell them you tried to stop Bobby from going, you don't want him there, all you want, all we want, is for him to come home?*

"Why don't you stand up for him, Mom?" I asked. *And for us,* I added to myself.

My mother turned to look at me, and I stared back at her, my arms crossed.

"Suzanne, I…" She had no words for me. She shook her head, looked away from me, stretched out her trembling fingers, then turned the key in the ignition.

I looked away from her too, I looked back at the store then, at the A&P, with all those protestors still waving their signs and shouting at the shoppers and the store manager, and I wanted to yell too, yell at those people, *you just don't understand. My mother has a son in Vietnam, too. And she tried, but couldn't stop his going.*

♦ ♦ ♦

"Hippies." My father spat out the word like I would broccoli. At the dinner table, it was me telling my father about the protestors at the grocery store, my mother's glance flitting everywhere around the kitchen as I told what happened.

"No-good troublemakers, with their long hair and peace signs. Why aren't they over there helping our boys, instead of staying here and stirring up trouble?" My father, done with his meal, tapped at the side of his empty coffee cup. "Our boys are sacrificing for everyone's freedom, just like my buddies and I did in World War Two, don't these protestors understand that?"

While my mother crossed the kitchen to get the coffee pot, I stayed at the table, tracking down the last grains of Rice-a-Roni with the tines of my fork. I didn't answer my father. I didn't have an answer for him. I only had a summer of no Bobby. No Bobby in the driveway, his head and shoulders gobbled up by the hood of the Chevy, saying, "Hand me that wrench, kiddo. And go see if Mom bought more Pepsi today and bring me one Suze. And get one for yourself, too, of course."

My father and his coffee cup settled in his recliner in the family room. Time for the news. Walter Cronkite's face filled the screen, and his rumbly voice filled my ears. God's twin, I always thought. I always thought that whatever Walter Cronkite

28

said in that deep, take-charge voice, that was the truth. The way it was. The way it had to be.

Walter Cronkite talked about the war, this battle, that offensive, as maps and photos flashed onto the screen over his shoulder. My father watched, listened, sipped his coffee. Then Walter came to the body count part.

My father stood up, walked the few steps to the TV, and clicked it off. He always turned off the news, silenced Walter, at the body count part. He never said why he did that. I could guess, but I knew my father would never say it.

"Why aren't we winning this war?" he said instead. To me? To the TV? I didn't know. "Any war is winnable. It's all these damn agitators. Our boys over there don't feel like they're supported; that's what it is."

Now my father looked right at me, and I thought about how he always talked about our boys in Vietnam, but never about Bobby. As if somehow Bobby didn't fall into that category. Or didn't deserve to be singled out in any special way.

"What about Bobby?" I asked my father.

My father fumbled in his shirt pocket for his pack of cigarettes. He pulled one of the white sticks out, tapped it against his finger. Tap tap.

"Bobby will be fine," my father answered me. "You know your brother. He's a likable kid. The way you and your mother fawn over him, you should know that better than anyone. But I'll bet this war is really shaping him up. Maybe he'll even sign up for a second tour of duty. Wouldn't surprise me. I knew if he just got a chance to get into the action, that boy would end up acting like a man. Like a real man. A man who takes action, fights for what's right."

I watched my father as he put the cigarette to his lips, flicked his lighter on, catching the round brown end in the flame, then sucked in, exhaled smoke. Did he notice yet that Bobby had written his first letters to me and Mom, but not to him? Did he notice anything about his son? He couldn't seem to decide which Bobby was, boy or man. Did he even know Bobby? He and Bobby used to play catch in the backyard, used to work on model cars together, patiently holding onto the glued-in little parts until they dried, but then Bobby got older, a teenager, a word my father seemed not even to like to say. And then there were no more model cars, just loud music and arguments about hair and oil drips in the driveway. Maybe he stopped knowing Bobby then. If he had ever known him at all.

I watched my father smoke his cigarette, and I thought about the times he would read to me, me on his lap, the book held out in front. My father never played with me much. I think his playing with Bobby used him up for me. Or maybe because I'm a girl, he didn't know what to play with me. But he did read to me. But now I couldn't remember how long ago it had been, the last time I sat in his lap. The last time my father and I really talked to each other. About anything.

I left my father in the family room and drifted down the hall, into Bobby's room, sat on his bed. My bare foot touched something hard and sharp, just under the bed. I bent down, pushed back the dust ruffle, picked the object up. The little metal Scottie dog from our Monopoly set.

I squeezed the little silver dog between my fingers and I smiled, remembering Bobby creeping into my room at night, calling softly, "Suze? Suzy-Q? Suzanne?" and then louder until I couldn't ignore him anymore and couldn't sleep anymore, and he wouldn't listen to me when I told him that it was a school night, I had to sleep. I would beg him to let me sleep, even get mad, but it wouldn't matter to Bobby. He knew once we started, once I really woke up, I wouldn't be mad anymore. Or at least not as much.

"Midnight Monopoly," he'd say, and I'd drag myself out of bed and across the hall to his room where he'd have the game all set up already. And I'd play, waking up more and more as the dice clattered onto the board making the little green houses and red hotels jump, and Bobby doled out the money, the banker, always.

Sometimes we didn't finish the game and it would be morning and so we would leave it set up and trust each other not to mess with the money and the property cards and the houses and the hotels, and my mother would say, "Oh, another midnight marathon Monopoly game," when she came by to wake us up. "You really should let Suzanne get her sleep, Bobby."

And then, "Bobby, couldn't you sleep last night? Again?"

I used to be woken up by Bobby for midnight Monopoly just once in a while, but then it turned into more games, more no-sleep nights for Bobby until I think the week before he left he didn't sleep at all. He didn't wake me up for Monopoly every night, but he did wake me up even with the softest strumming on his guitar. Even with the amp turned down to the lowest volume.

I set the little Scottie dog down on Bobby's dresser. I didn't know where the Monopoly set had been put away. Maybe in Bobby's closet, maybe in the linen closet beneath the extra towels. *I'll need to find it before Bobby gets back*, I thought. *He'll want to play.*

Next to Bobby's record player on the floor, between the turntable and the speakers, were his stacks of albums and 45s, all still in their jackets, protection against dust and scratches. Bobby took good care of his music. I flipped through the 45s, glanced at the album covers but didn't play any. Before he left, Bobby told me that I could use his record player, but I only liked Simon and Garfunkel really, and Bobby didn't have any of their records; I just had to sit near the radio and listen and wait for the "Sound of Silence" or the feeling groovy song—really it had another name I could never remember—to play.

"Suzanne. Bedtime."

My mother held a stack of folded laundry. *My mother's summer of laundry*, I thought again. She should have had less to do. With Bobby not there. No jeans stained with engine grease, no pile of sweaty tee shirts flung onto my brother's floor. But the laundry never stopped. My mother seemed determined to clean everything in the house, over and over.

"Suzanne, those protestors…"

"They didn't bother me," I interrupted. "Not really. I think…" I didn't finish. I didn't say what I thought. That they might be right. Might be doing the right thing.

My mother looked at me, and I looked at her, and I suddenly knew we were thinking the same thing about the protestors.

"But Mom, why didn't you tell them about Bobby?" I asked. "Really tell them?"

"Oh, Suzanne." My mother put a hand to her forehead, shook her head, same as in the morning. She didn't give me an answer.

I knew she wouldn't answer me. *It's because you're weak, Mom*, I thought. *Too weak to stand up for Bobby.*

Later, after teeth brushing and face washing, I laid between the sheets on my bed, thinking about that body count part on the news. *Or is it body part count*, I wondered. Either way I didn't like the way that part of the news tried to squeeze its way into my dreams at night, tried to keep me awake with pictures of body bags being carried down airplane steps.

"Don't watch the news, Suzanne," my mother told me, "if it bothers you so much." I knew my mother didn't watch, didn't want to see. But I had to know.

So then I had to lie in my bed at night, trying to sleep without dreams.

It's History

"Here, Suzanne," my mother said, setting pigs in a blanket and a glass of orange Tang in front of me. "Eat."

Tired of pigs in a blanket, I picked at the crust part with my thumbnail, revealing the layers below. Then I scraped the gooey cheese part out with my fingertip. The naked split-open hot dog, I picked up and ate. I didn't even take a sip of the warm orange Tang. I didn't like that chemical taste, the powder that didn't quite dissolve sticking to my tongue. We bought Tang because that's what the astronauts drank; maybe drinking Tang is the reason they were able to land on the moon. That's what you thought when you saw the Tang commercials on TV.

I remembered the night when I swirled the glass around, watched the bright orange Tang slosh against the sides. I had only wanted to sleep; I had tried, but my father kept shaking my shoulder, saying, "Suzanne, you have to come watch this, it's history, Suzanne," until finally I followed him to the family room, dragging my blanket with me, and crouched in front of the TV and watched the fuzzy black and white screen, the shapes that were supposed to be rocket ships and astronauts. The bulky white shape moving on the screen supposed to be Neil Armstrong, stepping onto the gray surface of the moon and saying his words, words we all waited for, or maybe my parents waited for—I just wanted to go back to my bed, my sleep.

My mother stood at the kitchen sink now, her hands and arms up to the elbows lost in the sudsy sink, while I picked away at my boring lunch. She scrubbed dishes, rinsed them, lifted them into the drying rack. My father didn't know that my mother never did the breakfast dishes until after lunch now.

That was okay; he was at work then. A talk show chattered out of the radio on the windowsill.

"What?" my mother suddenly asked, but not to me. She stuck a sudsy dish, not rinsed off, into the drying rack. She wiped her hands on her hips as she turned from the sink. She didn't look at me, she didn't look at anything. My mother ran to the front door, I heard her bang it open, but not close it behind her.

I bolted from my chair, hurried through dripped suds on the floor, to the window. I had to see what made my mother run out of the house. A toddler alone in the street, a truck bearing down on him? A child fallen from a bicycle, knees bleeding, crying?

I saw just a car. A parked car, not a car heading toward a child. But the car parked across the street at the Peretti's looked official somehow, squarish and dark. Just a parked car. But then I saw two official looking uniformed men standing on the Peretti's front porch. Staring at Mrs. Peretti's crumpled face.

Even from my across-the-street window, I could see Mrs. Peretti's face, could see that it had crumpled.

I watched my mother fly across the street, not bothering to look both ways. Not caring about cars careening toward her.

I turned away from the window, leaned back against the sink. I didn't want to watch anymore. I didn't want to see my mother hugging Mrs. Peretti as the official men left, didn't want to see the tears that would be sliding down both women's faces.

The Peretti's son, Tom, had shipped out, too. Went to Nam. Before Bobby.

I didn't know Tom very well. He had been older than Bobby. Way older than me.

My big toe found a sudsy bubble on the floor. I watched as the bubble popped around my toe, leaving that slippy slimy feeling on my skin.

I knew what had happened to Tom. I knew what it meant when two Army men came to your door. Two, so it wouldn't be just one who had to do the telling. Not just one to feel the blame. I wish I didn't know why they were at my neighbors' house. But I did.

And I also knew something else I didn't want to know. That now I would get older than Tom ever had a chance to be.

I cleared my lunch dishes from the table, dumped them into the sink, trying to help. I sat back down at the table, flipped through the newspaper, skipping the articles about the war, looking at ads for summer sandals and middle-of-the-season bathing suit sales.

My mother walked back into the house. No banging doors this time. I had flipped through the newspaper three times. I knew the comics from memory.

"Suzanne," my mother began. Her eyes were red, her skin blotchy.

"Tom died," I said, taking the words from her.

She nodded, crossed the kitchen to reach a cupboard, ignoring the dishes remaining in the sink. My mother pulled boxes and cans from the shelves, clattered them onto the counter. I watched her mix green powder into water, watched her open a can of miniature orange slices, then a can of peach parts. She dumped the fruit into the green Jell-O slush. She stirred briskly, too hard, as if her hands were angry at the fruit and the Jell-O.

"What else can I do, Suzanne?" she asked me. "What else?"

I didn't have an answer for my mother's question. I think she knew I didn't, but she had to ask it. "Why aren't we winning the war?" my father asked, and I didn't know. What could my mother do when the neighbor's son died in Vietnam? I didn't know that either.

But now I had a question. *Why? Why did Tom have to go? Why did he have to die there?*

My mother slid the pan into the refrigerator and returned to the dishes in the sink.

As she scrubbed and rinsed and jammed dishes into the rack, I walked into the living room, sat in the armchair next to the globe, picked up one of my mother's magazines from the magazine rack.

I read about cross-stitch patterns and toilet training toddlers and twelve uses for summer apricots. I read and read, although I didn't care about any of those things.

Several magazines later, my mother called me from the kitchen.

"Suzanne, I need you to do something for me. Please come here."

I knew what she wanted. I didn't want to do it. I didn't move. Maybe this time I would actually fight with my mother, argue with her, refuse to obey.

"No," I called. I wouldn't go. I wouldn't do it.

My mother walked into the living room, stood looking at me, her arms folded across her chest, too tight, as if she were holding her heart in. "Suzanne, please."

"I really don't want to, Mom," I said. "Why can't you do it?"

"This has been a very stressful day," my mother told me. "All I'm asking from you is a little help, Suzanne. A little consideration. You've been helping me this summer, and I really appreciate it, but I just need a little more help from you right now."

But why should I have to do it, Mom? I wondered. *Why should I have to do anything for you when you hardly do anything for me, with me, anymore?*

36

I threw the magazine down, heard the pages flutter, and stomped into the kitchen, after my mother.

"This isn't fair, Mom," I said. "Don't make me do it."

But she thrust the cold Jell-O dish into my hands anyway, as if she couldn't see me, or hear me, my anger at her request. "Please take this to the Peretti's, Suzanne. I need to lie down."

I took the pan. My mother left. I glared after her as she walked away from me.

Then I stared down through the clear plastic wrap at the orange pieces swimming through green. Someone dies in a war, and you give their family Jell-O.

But why not? Like my mother said, what else could she do?

I pushed the screen door open with my hip, and I walked down the driveway past piles of Chevy parts, and then across the street, not bothering to look for cars either, holding the cold pan out in front of me, chest high. I crossed the Peretti's front yard, past their trim rose bushes, avoiding the too-hot driveway with my bare feet.

I knocked on the screen door, heard a phone ringing inside, thought about leaving the pan on the front step and running, like a prank, like Devil's Night, the night before Halloween, but no, my mother would be upset. And how would the Perettis know where to return the pan?

I stood on the porch, and I waited, and then Janice opened the door, Tom's sister, bleary-eyed, a teenage sister.

She pushed open the screen door, held her hands out, knowing automatically what I offered.

"Thank you, Suzanne," she said as she lifted the pan from my hands. She didn't look at my face. I couldn't look at hers.

"I'm sorry," I said, but I mumbled it, and I didn't know if she heard me, if my mumbled sorry reached across the cold pan she now held.

"We're getting so much food," Janice said. "I'd rather have my brother."

I looked up, hearing the anger in her voice.

"Well, I guess at least we'll have his dog tags to remember him by," Janice said.

"What are you talking about?" I asked.

"Don't you know about the dog tags, Suzanne?" Janice asked me.

"Bobby told me in his first letter that they wear them, with their names on them," I replied. "Like name tags, I guess."

"Sure, name tags," Janice replied. "The names have to be on them so they can identify the guys when they're dead, Suzanne."

I stared at Janice. She stared back, her face hard, old tears dried on her cheeks.

I started to go, stepped backward, wanting to get away.

Then Janice turned toward her name being called from inside the house, and I escaped. I left, thinking Janice is, was, Tom's sister, and now she doesn't have a brother. Only his dog tags.

Bobby never told me that about the dog tags. He tried to make them sound funny. And so that's what I thought.

I tried not to think about dog tags as I crossed the Peretti's yard. *I won't think about them*, I told myself, *only about Bobby.*

Because I still had Bobby and when he came back he'd go across the street to talk to Janice; I knew he would, because he had been to Vietnam too, just like her brother. Bobby would be nice to Janice, and I wouldn't even mind if he gave her the first ride in the Chevy, when he finally got it running again.

I remembered the forgotten mail during my barefoot hot-pavement dance back across the street. A letter from Bobby lay on top of the pile in the mailbox; now I recognized the kind of ink, the stamp.

At first I wanted to run into the house and yell, *Mom, see, Bobby's okay, he's okay, he sent us another letter.* But then I thought, *she can wait for her letter. She made me go to the Perettis, she made me hear about dog tags. So she can wait until I've read my letter first.*

I tore into the envelope and pulled out my letter from Bobby, my letter on white lined paper, nestled inside of my mother's letter. I shook it open.

CHAPTER 7

My Letter First

"Dear Suzy-Q," I read. "If you think you have ever been hot, you have never been here. It's hotter and wetter than any place could ever be, and at the same time, too. There's rice fields spread out all over the place, so now I know where all that Rice-a-Roni you eat comes from. You should see the hats the rice farmers wear, straw and round, with a perfect point at the top. A little kid put one on my head while we were just messing around, and boy, it did cool my head off. But we're stuck with helmets, green, heavy, hot helmets, hotter than hell with the sun beating down on them all day. Funny thing is, I probably don't really need a helmet if my head's as hard as Dad always says it is."

I smiled, remembering Bobby rolling his eyes at my father's why-are-you-so-stubborn-all-the-time questions to him. More questions that no one ever answered, just my mother saying, "Now Jim, leave the boy alone," and "Bobby, pass your plate over here for some more mashed potatoes. And extra gravy." Always extra gravy for Bobby.

"We have to march, or crawl is more like it, through these wet fields, these rice paddies, and yesterday when we finally got out I had leeches stuck all over my skin, wherever I had bare skin showing. I stopped myself from screaming, but the guys still gave me a hard time because I had to pull those things off of me, and I really didn't like that. It's really hard to get these leeches off; they don't want to let go; they just want to keep sucking your blood. So when you pull them, they get all long and stretched out, and when you finally yank one off, it leaves blood dripping down your skin. I was totally grossed out, and the guys teased me, saying those leeches really like you, they must be in love with you Fishface—that's my nickname, I guess I forgot to tell you Suze that everyone gets a nickname here. The guys give it to you when you first arrive in country, and then you get so used to being called the nickname, that you practically forget your real name. And you forget the other guys' names too, even your best buddy's. I'm Fishface because I really complained about these rancid fish sticks they gave us my first night here, but also because the guys think I'm really ugly. Ha ha. (joke)."

That is funny, Bobby, I thought. No one would ever call Bobby ugly with those chocolate eyes and the way his smile would make you feel when he grinned at you, pleased by something you said or did. Even angry, even frowning, dark eyes flashing at you, Bobby looked good. His high cheekbones, strong jaw, chin spattered with missed whiskers. My brother always looked good. Even with hair down to his shoulders like a girl. Even now, with no hair, he still looked good, I knew. Girls always thought so too, at least since they were in seventh or eighth grade, but Bobby never had too much time for girls, for him it was always working on the Chevy and hanging out with his friends and playing his music. Except for Diane, when she started coming around, Bobby finally had a girlfriend, on and off, but not too serious. Bobby was never too serious about much, except his car and his songs.

"The thing about this war, Suzy, is that you can't ever tell who is on your side and who's not. I don't mean the guys in my company, I mean the Vietnamese. The people from the North, the ones we're fighting, look the same as the people from the South, the ones we're fighting with, and so anyone could be Viet Cong (that's the North ones) anytime. Anytime you set foot in the jungle or anytime you have to go down into one of the secret tunnels they have dug here all over the place, you don't know if you're going to face an enemy or not. You don't know if you're going to face a gun barrel or a mine ready for you to trip, ready to blow you up. I have to tell you, Suze, I made a good buddy when I got here, but I lost him to a tunnel last week. I mean, he's dead. They sent his body, or what was left of it, home. But me, I'm still all in one piece, hard head and all. And that's the way I'm planning on coming home."

"Are you having fun this summer, Suzy-Q? Are you going to the pool? Make sure Mom doesn't worry too much. It doesn't do any good anyway. Oh, before I left I told Rob that he could borrow my Dylan albums if he wants to, until I get back. I also told him he could get a job to buy his own albums. Ha ha. Seriously, those college boys have it too good, but I don't fault Rob for that. I guess I could have been planning to go, started this summer like Rob did, but grades just were never my thing. So if he comes around, let him have whatever albums he wants, and I'll get them when I get back. He'll only have them for a year, or really less now. A year isn't that long, Suze, but it's sure longer here.

"We heard on the radio about the moon landing, and I looked up into the sky later, when it got dark here, and it seemed too hard to believe that the same moon was hanging over me here and you there, Suzy, you there out in the back catching those lightning bugs at night."

Lightning bugs. I hadn't looked for them all summer that year. I never was that good at catching them anyway. Bobby could fill a jar full while I only caught two or three, each one fluttering between my almost closed palms until I scraped it off of my hand and into the jar, quickly tightening the lid, punched with air holes, back on. Lots of kids liked to keep those jars in their rooms all night to watch the blinking yellow lights as they fell asleep, and then the jar would be full of dead lightning bugs littering the bottom in the morning. But Bobby always said we had to let ours go when Mom called us in at night. How would you like to be stuck in a jar to die, he asked me, no chance to escape. I wouldn't like that at all, Bobby, I would agree, even though I really wanted to have a blinking jar next to my bed as I fell asleep. But I knew he was right, and so we always set our bugs free, both of us unscrewing our jar lids at the same time, coaxing the last bugs out, back into the dark sky surrounding us.

I read the "So long, Suze," at the bottom of my letter and folded it back up, and then I carried my mother's letter down the hallway. I walked into her darkened room and saw that she was awake and sitting up. I handed her the letter and I said, "Bobby's okay still. He's okay."

And then I sat on the end of my mother's bed while she read the letter and rested some more, and I turned on the TV in her room, let the afternoon cartoons wash over me, silently, the sound turned off, my mother's way of watching becoming my way too.

CHAPTER 8

Box Hockey King

My days with Bobby gone were box hockey days down at the school. It was my last summer to go to the summer day camp; the next year, after sixth grade, I'd be too old. Summer days dragging, I wheeled my bike out of the garage, wiped the dust from the seat with one finger, and pedaled the few blocks to the school.

Inside, in the cafeteria, the long tables with attached benches were pulled out of the walls, rows of our lunch tables and benches filled the room. Kids, kindergarten age and up, kneeled or swiveled on their bottoms on the smooth benches. High school age, maybe college age, counselors, supervised the crafts, the giving out of popsicles, the sitting-in-a-circle song singing or kickball game outside.

Inside I spotted Kathy and Mary Ann at one of the tables, braiding gimp.

"Hi Suzanne." Kathy looked up as I approached the table. "I'm glad you've finally come down here. Look what we're making."

Kathy held up her project, a chain of braided gimp, that long stringy plastic that came in every bright color, for making necklaces and key chains.

"She's making that for Ricky," Mary Ann told me, and giggled.

"Shut up, I am not," Kathy insisted, her skin threatening to pinken.

I slid onto the seat next to Kathy. I didn't like Mary Ann. She thought she was old; she acted too old; I saw her smoking cigarettes in the bathroom at the ice skating rink right before they closed it for the season last March. Mary Ann thought that boys were impressed that she had a chest. She didn't know that most of the boys our age were still too interested in baseball cards and model cars to care.

I fingered the strands of gimp on the table in front of me, debating on whether to make a necklace, key ring, or nothing.

"So do you ever hear from your brother?" Kathy asked me as she wove together two strings, pink and purple.

"He writes us letters," I said. "He's doing okay."

"I think it's so romantic that he went to the war," Mary Ann said. "I bet when he gets back there will be all these girls after him. Maybe he'll get his picture in the paper kissing some girl like that famous one from that other war. You guys know which one I mean?"

I nodded. I knew which photograph she meant, the one from my father's war, but all I could think about was that word Mary Ann used, romantic. So far nothing in Bobby's letters had made me think of that word.

"So do you think he'll get a parade, Suzanne?" Kathy asked as she held up her gimp creation for inspection.

A parade? "I don't think so," I answered her. "I don't think they do that anymore."

"Too bad." Kathy shrugged.

Tom Peretti didn't get a parade, I thought. All I saw the Perettis get was an endless parade of cars parking in front of their house, an endless parade of people in dark clothes emerging from the cars and trooping in and out of the house. And lots of pans of food, tuna casseroles and Jell-O salad.

"Are you going to make something, Suzanne?" Mary Ann asked me.

"No." I stood up. "I don't think so. I think I'll go outside."

"You're not going to start on that box hockey thing again, are you, Suzanne?" Kathy asked. Kathy turned to Mary Ann and explained. "Last summer practically all Suzanne did here was play box hockey. She even brought her own stick from home."

Mary Ann and Kathy laughed, and I remembered the stick, the box hockey stick that Bobby sawed and sanded from a thick wooden dowel. "When I was your age," he told me, "I was box hockey king at that school, and I want you to follow in my footsteps, Suze. You have to have your own stick. Who wants to use a stick sweaty from every other kid's hands and splintered from the sore losers slamming it down against that stone porch? Here you go, Suze," and he handed me my own smooth box hockey stick, and I used it the summer before every day at day camp, but I couldn't remember where I put it when that summer ended. Somewhere in the garage, probably. Unless Bobby used it to hold up the hood on the Chevy this past spring. Then maybe it's been stashed in the trunk or the back seat of his car. I'll have to look in the car, and in the garage and see if I can find it, I decided.

"Well?"

Kathy and Mary Ann were looking at me, and it was my turn to shrug. "Maybe," I answered. "Maybe I will."

And then I turned away and walked past the tables, past tables where kids glued popsicle sticks together to make square boxes and little log cabins with the roof sticks sliding off unless you held them in place for a long time to let the glue dry, and past tables where kids rolled magazine pages into tight little cylinders and pasted them onto the outside of orange juice cans to make ugly pencil holders for their parents' desks.

I pushed against the bar on the heavy front door and emerged onto the porch. The box hockey line snaked along the porch, around the columns, and onto the pavement path. And I thought, *Maybe I will play.* I wanted to feel one of those wooden sticks

46

in my hand, wanted to feel the smack smack smack of the box hockey stick vibrate into the palm of my hand and up my arm, almost to the elbow.

But in one corner of the porch, near the brick wall, two kids stood flipping baseball cards, and that caught my attention. I watched them for several minutes, each kid with a stack of graying-at-the-edges cards held tight in his hand, each kid taking a turn to flip his top card toward the wall. Then the other kid flipped his and if it matched the one lying on the porch, either the front side photo of the player facing up or back side with the player's stats, then he got to keep both cards, scooping them up and adding the cards to his pile. If his card didn't match the other one, then the first flipper kept both.

I had a shoebox full of baseball cards at home, up high on the shelf in my closet. Whenever I used to get the box down and carry it out to the kitchen table so I could lay them all out on a flat surface, my mother would sigh and say, "Suzanne, can't you ever do anything feminine? The way you're always helping Bobby with that car, I'm afraid you'll grow up to be a grease monkey." But I wouldn't put the cards away, not until I felt like it, and sometimes Bobby would still trade with me from his own shoebox, if I really begged him to, even though he was old, already in high school, too old to care about baseball cards. "This is boring, Suzanne," he'd say, "I've got things to do, I've got to meet Rob and Jack." And then he'd leave, leave me alone with all the cards. But sometimes he would stay and sort through the cards with me, and we'd compare the players' stats, Clemente and Stargell, our favorites, their batting averages and RBIs, and Bobby would say we need to go to a Pirates game soon, Suze, and once we even went, taking the trolley downtown and walking together to the stadium. I still had the pennant I bought that day, tacked onto the wall above my bed.

I joined the box hockey line and waited for my turn, listening to the smacking sounds of sticks hitting the wooden sides of the box, hitting the stones of the porch. And the cheering from kids in line, for their friends, or just cheering, hoping to speed up the games' ends, get their own turns sooner.

Finally my turn: I took the stick handed to me, grasped it, felt the sweatiness and the splinters pricking my skin, and took my place at the side of the box.

My opponent, the last winner, a boy I recognized from a year behind me in school but didn't know, placed the round black puck on top of the center board, and we crouched, touched sticks to the ground in opposite sides of the box.

Then smack, we brought our sticks up, they met in the air, once, twice, three times, the smacks ringing across the porch, and then the game began, and I flew after that puck. I jammed it through one of the center holes, toward my goal, and then battled that kid, stick against stick, and the wooden sides of the box, until finally I forced the puck through the hole at my end and it hit the shoe of someone waiting in line.

The kid I beat tossed down his stick, and I was the winner, and so the next kid in line had to play against me, and I won again. The line moved, mostly boys, some girls, mostly kids I knew from school, some I didn't. I kept winning.

"No one can beat Suzanne," one kid said to the others fidgeting behind him in that long snaky line.

My fingers stung from being smacked by the other sticks, by accident during the wild box hockey battles, and a blister started to form on my thumb, but I kept playing. I played kids twice, three times, and I never lost.

"Suzanne's in a fighting way," Steve, a kid from my grade, said as I won another game in my endless string of victories.

I wiped my sweaty hand on the side of my shorts, and I looked at Steve and thought, *Maybe I am.*

And I was still winning when two teenage counselors came through the front door, one calling, "Three o'clock. Time to pack it in," and I had to hand over my stick and watch the counselors drag the heavy wooden box back inside, locked in for the night.

I blew on my hot blistered fingers, hoping to cool them off, and thought about Bobby being box hockey king and his footsteps and wondered where his footsteps were taking him right then. And would I ever know, could I ever understand, no matter how much he told me about jungles and tunnels and losing buddies? And I was glad to be box hockey king too, just like my brother, even if only for one day.

CHAPTER 9

Rob and Diane

I thanked Mrs. Wilson for the ride as I got out of the car at the end of my driveway, waved to Kathy, agreed to call her soon, agreed that we had fun at the pool. I stood in the driveway, watched the Plymouth back out into the street, wrapped my damp towel around my waist, and tugged at the bottom of my too-small suit beneath the towel.

I turned around, faced the house, faced Bobby's Chevy. I walked up to my brother's car and placed my water-wrinkled fingertips on the chipped blue paint on the hood. The metal, sun-warmed, felt hot, but not too hot to touch. I let both of my palms rest on the hood of Bobby's Chevy.

Then I heard a car driving on the street behind me, but I didn't turn around. Probably someone going to visit the Perettis, a friend of Janice's, a bridge partner of Mrs. Peretti. But then I heard my name as the car engine died, a deep voice calling, a voice like Bobby's.

"Suzanne!"

I whirled around toward my name, heard two car doors slamming. I watched Rob and Diane walking toward me from Rob's Nova parked on the street. The twin to my brother's car, but brand new. My brother's was a first year model, and other owners used it hard before it became Bobby's car. Rob's car had no rust patches, no dents, and unchipped red, not blue paint. Bobby's best friend crossed the driveway toward me, walking with Diane, Bobby's sometimes girlfriend, sometimes not. Diane smiled at me as they reached me and adjusted her halter top, a triangle of purple fabric covering her chest.

"We were just driving around and thought we'd stop by and see what you hear from Bobby," Rob explained.

"He sends us letters," I replied. "Doesn't he write to you two?"

"Not often," Rob said. He shrugged. "Well, only once to me so far. So I thought you might tell us what's happening with him."

"He's in a war," I told them.

Rob and Diane exchanged glances, but why did they bother, they wore identical expressions anyway. They both looked back at me, Diane shaking her head.

"Suzanne, why do you have to be like that?" Diane asked. "I know Bobby usually thinks you're just the greatest kid to walk the face of the earth, except when you're being annoying, like right now. But to me you seem..."

Honest? I thought as Diane bit off her words, not wanting to insult me, I guess, the soldier's little sister.

"Maybe he doesn't write to you because he doesn't think you'd understand," I said.

Rob lifted the hem of his black tee shirt to his face, wiping sweat from his nose and chin, exposing a belly button surrounded by black curly hair. Then he let the crumpled tee shirt fall back into place, covering his stomach and the waistband of his jeans.

"Look Suzanne, I know I'm not there so maybe I don't understand," Rob said. "But it's not my fault that I got a college deferment and Bobby got stuck. I wouldn't trade places with him for a million bucks, but I sure wish he hadn't gone. I'm sure you wish he hadn't gone too, but does that mean that you're going to hate everyone who didn't go to Vietnam?"

I had never thought of that. I didn't hate anyone. I just hated the fact that my brother had to go fight in a war, and I hated the unfairness that let Rob stand in the driveway alive, across the street from dead Tom's house.

"I don't want anyone to go to Vietnam," I said.

"Are you a dove, Suzanne?" Diane asked.

I stared at Diane, at her long straight corn-colored hair flowing past her bare shoulders and almost down to her faded jeans, and then my eyes trailed down the length of those jeans to the painted toenails peeking out from her clunky brown sandals.

"What do you mean?" I asked.

"You know, a dove, a person who wants peace, who wants us to get out of Vietnam," Diane explained. "As opposed to hawks. Those are the people who support the war, who want to send our men over there to fight in it."

I remembered the protestors at the A&P and my father calling them hippies like that was a swear word, and I looked from Diane's flat hair and faded jeans to Rob, whose dark curly hair had been growing out, covering his ears, almost reaching chin length, and whose jeans ended in a tattered frayed edge.

And I thought about my father, who only talked about Bobby doing his part like he was an actor in a play reciting lines; who talked about the war as if it were a football game, and our side could win if they just ran the right plays.

"I don't know," I finally answered. "I don't know anything about hawks and doves. I just want Bobby to come home."

"That's all we want too, Suzanne," Rob said.

"Okay," I said. "I'm sorry I acted like that." And I was. Like Rob said, it wasn't his fault. "In his last letter, Bobby said you could borrow his Bob Dylan albums until he comes back, if you want to, Rob." I offered Bobby's best friend what I could of my brother, until we could all have him back.

"Hey, that's cool, Suzanne," Rob said. "But actually, between the two of us, Diane and I have all of Dylan's albums. But thanks anyway."

I heard the words the two of us and I looked at Bobby's best friend and his on-and-off girlfriend and, I realized that things here were just like one of Bobby's favorite Dylan songs, the

"Times They Are A-Changin'." While Bobby lost buddies in tunnels in Vietnam, Rob and Diane were teaming up over here. I guess not everything could stay the same while Bobby was away. I wondered what he would say about Rob and Diane when he came home. I started to wonder how different things would seem to him when he came home, and then I started to wonder if he would seem different too. I wondered if when my brother came back, if I would get the same brother back. Or not.

Rob slapped the hood of the Chevy. "I could come over some time and see what I can do with this old heap," he offered.

I shook my head, but smiling, friendly. "That's okay, Rob. I always help Bobby with it, and I know he wants us to fix it together."

Diane reached out and pressed a finger to my shoulder. "Better get out of the sun soon, Suzanne. You're getting a nasty sunburn."

I nodded, agreeing, as Rob and Diane told me goodbye and so long and see you later and walked to Rob's car, opened the doors and slipped inside. I saw their hands touch before Rob started the engine, and as the car pulled away from the curb, I couldn't help but feel that the people inside of it were pulling away from the curb and Bobby at the same time.

I didn't want my brother to lose everybody on both sides of the world, but I didn't know how to stop that from happening. How do you keep people from slipping away from you? Or from being blown into little bits in front of you? I knew all that stuff, about bombs and grenades; I read the newspaper; I watched the news. But not for answers. I wanted answers, but all I ever got were more questions.

I kicked my rubber thongs off of my feet as I walked into the house. Kathy and I had stayed late at the pool, jumping off the low dive and lying on our spread-out towels eating frozen

Milkshake bars. My father already stood in the kitchen, the sleeves of his white shirt rolled up, his drink already gripped in one hand. Ice was floating in the clear liquid.

"How was swimming, Suzanne?" My mother stopped slicing carrots at the counter to ask me, too interested. I knew I had interrupted something, something my parents didn't want me to know.

"Fine," I said, sitting down, using my towel as a cushion. "What's going on? Is it something about Bobby?"

"Nothing," my father said. "Nothing to concern yourself about, Suzanne."

"Suzanne, your father wants us to go a rally on Monday," my mother told me, slowly, chopping her words into pieces just like she sliced the orange carrot coins.

"What do you mean, a rally?" I asked. "What kind of rally?"

"A war rally. To support our troops, of course," my father said, but looking at my mother, not at me. "What kind did you think?"

My father set his glass down on the counter, too hard, and the bang made my mother's shoulders lift, startled. "Call me when dinner's ready," he said as he walked out of the kitchen.

My mother paused in her slicing, and she looked at me. I hadn't looked at her, really looked, for a while. I noticed that her hair had become kind of scraggly, as if she hadn't set it in curlers the night before. And she didn't wear a dress, she wore the kind of stained stretch pants she only wore for scrubbing the bathrooms, her comfy pants, she called them, and I remembered how she always used to freshen herself up, as she would say, before my father arrived home.

But she didn't look fresh now, and I thought she was about to tell me something about the rally, but she didn't. She turned and looked at me, really looked, into my eyes with hers, but she didn't say anything about the rally and what my father had said.

And she didn't say anything about how things seemed different in my family now, my mother and father not acting right, not like before. *When Bobby gets back, will we be the same family?* I wondered. I wanted my mother to tell me what was happening here, but I didn't ask, afraid of the answer, and I knew she probably wouldn't tell me anything anyway.

"Wash your hands and set the table now, please," she said instead.

And I did as she asked, prepared our table for our family dinner, where I knew no one would say much of anything, and especially not the word that caused the tension in my parents' kitchen that day. That the word, *rally*, would hang over the three of us like a bomb about to explode.

CHAPTER 10

What I'm Doing Here Isn't Right

"I can't even pronounce the names around here," my brother wrote. "I won't even try. We just hump from one village to the next, through bug-infested swamps and rice paddies, past huts and more huts, searching for the Cong. About all we ever find are little naked children, some of them missing an arm or a leg, scraping in the dirt in front of their burned out huts, and old toothless women sitting out in front watching them and watching us.

"And dead bodies. Dead women and dead children and dead people who had nothing to do with this war. Just people trying to live their lives. They didn't ask for us to be here, bombing and burning their villages, their homes.

"And so we just walk and search and never know when we might set off a trap, maybe blow up our own buddies.

"Suze, I don't want to watch any more of my buddies die. Or lose their arms or legs or eyes or their minds. I don't want to kill people I never even met before, never even heard of, and don't have a thing against.

"Don't tell Dad, kiddo, but I've changed. I'm even worse than he used to think of me. I thought I knew why I was coming to Nam. I thought there was a point to it. I thought it was right. I thought it was like Dad said, that I had a part to play in this. But now, it's different. I'm different. I don't know about the politics of it, but I do know that what I'm doing here isn't right. This war has nothing to do with me. This war shouldn't even be happening. I don't really know what I'm doing here anymore, except for trying to stay alive.

"I just want to come home. I'm keeping my head low, so far so good, and counting the days till the end of my tour.

"Sorry this letter is such a downer, Suzy-Q. It's hard to stay up in a place like this. But I still have that picture on me, you know, the one of me and you when you were just learning to ride your bike, and I let go for the first time and Dad took the picture at just the right moment, for once luckily he was using the regular camera instead of the movie camera. That expression on your face, kiddo, there's nothing better than that. I look at that picture sometimes, and I don't know, somehow it helps.

"Hey, if Rob borrows my Dylan albums like he said he might, tell him I want them back when I get home, okay, Suze?"

Okay, Bobby, I promised, even though I knew Rob wouldn't be borrowing the albums, might not be coming around at all for a while.

I smoothed out the letter, slipped it into my-empty-except-for-Bobby's-letters scrapbook. *When he comes home*, I thought, *I'll take the letters out, not needing them anymore, and fill the scrapbook with school pictures of friends and ticket stubs and science-fair blue ribbons, like you're supposed to.*

Bobby wants to come home, I thought. *He doesn't want to stay; won't sign up for another year like my father thought he might. And if he wants to come home, he will.* I smiled. My big brother always got what he wanted before, his guitar and his car and tickets to the Rolling Stones concert. So why not now?

CHAPTER 11

The Rally

"We're going because your brother is over there," my father had an answer to one of my questions, why do we have to go? "Because we support him."

My mother and I said nothing. Our thighs and backs stuck to the hot sticky seats in the station wagon, we were encased in polyester shorts and matching striped sleeveless shirts—my father's insistence on proper clothes for a Labor Day outing. We were going because my father said we had to. My mother and I hadn't discussed not wanting to go, but I knew how she felt. She felt just like me. *So why don't you say something, Mom?* I wanted to say. *Why don't you refuse to go?* But I said nothing, just stared at the back of my mother's neck as we sped along the highway.

The rally filled the park. "USA All The Way" read the signs draped across the roofs of the picnic shelters. "America—Love It Or Leave It" signs planted in the grass. American flags rippled in the breeze.

My father parked the car, grabbed the grocery sack stuffed with bags of Fritos and Ruffles and Lays. My mother carried the Jell-O salad.

My tight white sandals carried my feet through the grass, toward a picnic shelter. People were spilling out of the open sides, smoke drifting from the grill. My parents set their offerings on a picnic table next to pans of potato salad and tuna salad and other colors of Jell-O salad, more potato chips and pickle chips; there were hot dogs and there were real dogs gobbling up the fallen scraps beneath the tables.

I watched my father greet other men gathered at the rally, shaking hands with other men also dressed in their casual clothes, pressed slacks and button down shirts with the sleeves rolled up. Black shined shoes, as always.

"We've got to show that we support our boys," my father told the men, who nodded, agreed with him, responded with their own comments. "When we fought in World War Two, this country stood behind us," my father continued. "We've got to do that this time, too. People try to say this is a different kind of war, but it's not. It's all about freedom. About America. And winning."

"They just need more firepower to kill those gooks," one man explained. "Then we'll win."

The men nodded, agreed, smiled, happy to be with others who agreed with them, their own kind, happy to agree about killing gooks.

My mother perched on a picnic bench, stared down, tracing the raised seams on the front of her shorts with her fingertips. A woman approached her, holding out a miniature American flag on a stick, offering.

My mother shook her head, but smiled. A little. Politely. "No, thank you," she said. "I'd rather not."

The woman walked on, offering her flags, and my mother looked over at me. "Suzanne, why don't you go join that badminton game?" she suggested.

I glanced across the lawn at the group of kids chasing the little plastic birdie with their skinny racquets, heard their shrieks at misses, gloats at good shots.

I shook my head. "I'd rather not." Echoing my mother's words, identical like our outfits. My mother didn't smile at me, but I knew she understood.

The rally people milled around one another, around my mother and me. They gathered food on paper plates and traded comments, remarks about the war and our boys and the picnic shelter filled with laughter and chatter until suddenly those sounds stopped, almost at once, as everyone turned toward a new sound bombarding us from the parking lot.

The sound came from battered VW vans and Beetles and other dirty, rusted vehicles screeching into the parking lot, stopping wherever they felt like it, skipping the between-the-lines routine. And from car doors opening, releasing people clothed in torn jeans and tie-dye tee shirts and bandanas holding back the hair. Always the hair, sometimes long and flat, sometimes bushy and wild shooting out from their scalps like an explosion.

My father stood next to me, staring hard at the group gathering in the parking lot. He snorted. "Look at that. Hippies. Longhairs. With their peace signs and love beads. Cowards who won't fight like your brother."

Signs were handed out, passed around, the people spread in front of the parked cars, held their signs up, and began to chant.

"End The War," I read the painted-on words. And "Stop The Killing," I read. And I listened to the "Get Out Of Vietnam" chant.

I stared across the lawn, stared at the protestors as I gave them that name, and realized what they were protesting. The rally. Us. Me.

"Get a job!" my father shouted.

Other people gathered in the picnic shelter joined my father in shouting. The badminton game abandoned, the kids shouted too.

The protestors chanted. The rally goers shouted.

I'm on the wrong side, I thought. *So is my mother. My mother and I don't belong on this side. I don't want to be here. I can't be here.*

I looked over at my mother watching me, not the protestors.

"I'm going over there, Mom," I said. "Come with me."

No, my mother shook her head no.

"Mom, come on," I almost felt like shouting at my mother, shouting at her to do something, to act the way she felt, the way we felt. "Come with me."

"I can't, Suzanne," she said. "I just can't."

I didn't care then. I would go alone. Leave her here.

I stepped off the concrete floor of the picnic shelter, stepped onto the grass. I crossed the lawn spread between the shelter and the parking lot. I waited for my father's grasp on my shoulder, waited for his shout of Suzanne, get back here.

Neither came. I reached the parking lot, approached the protesting group. My father hadn't stopped me. Maybe he didn't see me. Maybe he couldn't see me, the same way I knew he couldn't really see Bobby.

"What do you want?" a long hair asked me. I didn't wear his kind of clothes. I came from the other side. Maybe he thought I was a hawk, coming to hurt his flock of doves.

"A sign," I told him. "I'm on your side."

A smile, a rustle in the group, words beneath the chants and a sign appeared, was handed to me. "Bring Our Boys Home" in big black letters. I held it, smiled, too. Perfect.

I held my sign high, chanted, stared across the parking lot at my parents. After a while, the shouters, giving up, or thinking they could win by ignoring their enemies, went back to their picnic food and picnic games.

Only my mother still sat and watched. Watched me and the group I had joined.

I didn't know if my father would be angry. No, I knew. I didn't know how angry he would be, what he would do. And I didn't know who was right or who was wrong in that place, that sliver on the globe, called Vietnam. I only knew that anything that took my brother away and maybe never gave him back, had to be wrong. Anything that turned my plaid and purple summer into dreams of body parts, and parents who could barely speak to each other, was wrong.

The sign I held was heavy. The wood was splintered, not smooth to the touch. The chanting tore at my throat, made my voice raw. But I knew, if holding a sign would help bring Bobby back, just like he promised, I would hold that sign until that day happened. And, I knew, even when my brother came home, I'd still hold that sign. Forever, if I had to. Until everybody's brother came home.

I held my sign as the sky darkened and the fireworks began. Set off by the rally people, not-even-dark-yet fireworks. Way past the Fourth of July fireworks. Red, white, and blue fireworks. Bobby-gone-to-Nam fireworks.

I looked up into the sky, watched the fireworks exploding above me, thought they looked like bruises in the sky. I thought they looked like what Bobby saw when his buddies set off a trap. A bomb. A boom, and spray of colors. Blood red, blinding white, sorrow blue.

The fireworks ended, the rally people began to drift toward their cars. I handed my sign to the protestor standing next to me and headed toward our station wagon.

In the back seat, on the now cooled-off vinyl, I waited for the click of the front doors opening. I heard the click. Then my father's face appeared over the front seat. With narrowed eyes, frowning mouth, he glared at me.

"I didn't stop you because I didn't want everyone there to know that you were my daughter," my father told me. He shook his head, his slicked down hair not loosening by even a strand. "I have only one thing to say to you, Suzanne. I am ashamed of you. Your brother is in Vietnam, for God's sake!"

I looked away from my father, out the window, at angry faces shouting at one another again, but closer to one another now, and I thought, *Well Dad, I only have one thing to say to you.*

Exactly.

CHAPTER 12

Refuse To Be Silenced

My parents fought. About me. About my punishment. My mother, who had never yelled at my father before, yelled. "She did the right thing, Jim," she yelled. "She stood up for her beliefs. And for her brother."

"I don't want to hear any more of this peacenik crap, Marna," my father yelled back. "Suzanne needs to be punished for turning against her brother."

I jammed my head beneath my pillow, suffocated my parents' words. I had never really been punished before. I had never really disobeyed. And I hadn't really disobeyed at the rally. No one told me not to go over to the other side. But my heart had told me to. My heart is what I obeyed. And I did it for Bobby. I would do anything to bring Bobby back.

I didn't hear the rest of the argument, the fight, my head buried beneath thick cotton and foam. But my mother must have gotten her way. Somehow. I was never punished; the rally was never even mentioned again.

My parents stopped mentioning much of anything to each other after that.

And neither of them told me anything about us, our family. What was happening to us. I didn't want my family to change this way; I wanted us to be the same for Bobby when he got back. *Would we even be a family?* I wondered. *Would he even have anything to come back to?*

But I didn't say anything about it, either. My mother and I didn't feel the way my father did. Nothing would change that. Could change that.

My mother did say some things, things like asking my father for the credit card, to go shopping. Suzanne needs new school clothes, she explained to my father. And he handed over the card.

But my father wouldn't look at what we bought. No back-to-school fashion show that year. He used to say nice, very nice, as I paraded my new outfits in front of him. And only sometimes asking, "How much did that cost, Marna?" But this time he looked away from us, away from our arms filled with bags from the mall, crossed the room, turned up the volume on the TV to hear "Love American Style" better, to hear us worse.

My father wouldn't look at my peace sign tee shirts, my bell bottomed jeans, my flat, growing out hair. They made him mad.

My mother's dangling peace sign earrings made him madder. *You're mad about the wrong things, Dad,* I thought. *Why aren't you mad about Bobby?* I wanted to ask, but wouldn't. My father and I used to talk; he used to tease me and beat me at checkers, pounding his kings across the board, but now, he didn't talk to me much, sometimes not at all. *I'm not even a teenager,* I thought, but that's not it, I knew. I felt a line through my family, a wall that no one crossed, a wall that started being built before Bobby left, that now reached so high, we couldn't even see across it, let alone reach across it. So I didn't ask my father another question he couldn't or wouldn't answer.

School started; I did my homework, rushed to the mailbox, racing my mother. Every letter brought Bobby one more letter closer to home.

"Do you want to help?" my mother asked me, the drips dangling from her paintbrush. "I could really use the help, your help, Suzanne." She smiled at me, an actual smile.

My mother, in the garage, used a saw for the first time. And nails and sandpaper. And her signs were good, strong. I picked up a paintbrush.

My mother and I painted words, and I thought, *Hey, now I have an answer to one question.* My mother's what else can I do question from the day of Tom and Jell-O salad.

We can paint words on signs and tell the world what we think. What we really think. We can shout and scream and be heard. We can try to change things.

My mother shopped on Friday evenings now, after my father brought the car home from work. After she warmed up a can of soup for dinner or made chicken salad sandwiches. My father didn't ask where his meatloaf and mashed potato dinners were. He didn't ask about anything, just ate and settled in front of the TV. Poured his own coffee.

Saturday mornings, my mother and I drove to the A&P. We wore matching outfits, jeans and tee shirts, tie-dyed colors splashed across our chests, matching the group we joined each time, blending in, matching clothes, matching feelings. We held signs, we chanted. The manager, with his threats of police, or real police pulling into the parking lot in their squad cars, would scatter us off of the property, onto public space around the edges. We didn't want to be arrested. We just wanted to be heard.

But before the manager called or the police came, we stood in front of angry shoppers, angry at us as their ice cream melted in their carts.

It's okay, I wanted to tell the shoppers. *Summer's over. You can get by without ice cream.*

Kathy and her mother emerged from the A&P, Kathy pushing a loaded cart through the magic doors, her mother clicking her purse shut.

"Marna!" Mrs. Wilson exclaimed, stopping. The cart just missed ramming into her ankles as Kathy stopped too.

"What are you doing?"

"Stopping the war," my mother replied. "Trying to."

Kathy and her mother looked at each other, then back to us, examining our jeans, our not-done at the beauty parlor hair. Finally Kathy spoke to me.

"But your brother's there," she said.

"Exactly," I said, finally out loud, wanting to shout it. *That's exactly why I'm doing this.*

"The kids at school are going to think this is really weird," Kathy warned me. "They're already wondering about you, Suzanne."

I shrugged. *What did that matter?* I thought.

"Who's going to tell them?" I asked.

Kathy shrugged, mimicking me. "People hear things. You know how stuff gets around."

"Well, Marna, will you be joining our Friday afternoon bridge club when we finally get it going this fall?" Mrs. Wilson asked my mother.

"I don't know," my mother answered. "I don't have much time now."

"I'll call you," Mrs. Wilson said, grabbing the cart and steering it and Kathy past us.

We let them through. We let everyone through, but first they had to face our signs, hear what we had to say. Whether they wanted to listen or not.

At school, no one wanted to listen. At school, the kids and the teachers wanted to be deaf to the war.

In the other sixth grade class, a new girl named Tracy didn't come to school. For several days, then a week. Then more. On the playground, kids relayed the whispered rumor of a death in the family. A rumor in code. Everyone knew that Tracy's brother had gone to Vietnam before her family moved here. Just like they knew that my brother had gone, too. But no one would say who died in Tracy's family. Even though we all knew. The teachers only said "Open your math books to page sixty-three," and, "Write the report in cursive, please."

I thought we should shout it out, tell everyone, shout out that Tracy's brother had been killed in the Vietnam War and what are we going to do about it, what are we going to do about the other brothers who are still there?

But if I tried to speak, it was, "Shh, open your math book, Suzanne, let's not talk about that here."

On the playground, at recess, Ricky and Kevin and Steve hanging upside down from the monkey bars, lacking only bananas, chanted at me as I walked by.

"If I die in a combat zone, box me up and ship me home," they chanted. I stopped to watch them, tried to think of what to say, what to tell them that could matter to them, make them see.

"Watch out," Steve called. "Box hockey Suzanne is heading our way."

The three boys climbed higher, perched on the top of the monkey bars, pretending fear, pretending I would do them harm if I clutched box hockey sticks in my hands.

"Don't worry, guys," Ricky said. "Suzanne's a peacenik now. She can't beat us up."

I stared up at the boys on the monkey bars, thinking, *Maybe I am a peacenik now, but maybe I'm still just Suzanne. All I really am is a girl who wants her brother to come home.* And even though I didn't like the boys on the monkey bars very much, I didn't want any of them to be sent to this endless war that kept dragging on. Dragging our childhoods through the mud and muck along with it.

I walked away from the monkey bars, leaving the monkeys on top shooting at me with their imaginary guns, rat-a-tat-tats blowing from their lips.

I wandered across the playground, not wanting to join the games of tetherball and four square that my friends, or used-to-be friends, were playing, didn't want to join the clusters of girls gossiping about who liked whom. I climbed the worn grass hill that sloped toward the school, toward the front porch where summer box hockey games were played, and I saw, sitting on the stones of the porch, Miss Von Schlott, a fourth grade teacher, strumming a guitar.

I heard notes, familiar notes, and as I walked nearer, I heard familiar words.

"How many miles must a man walk down before they will call him a man?" Miss Von Schlott sang words that I had heard Bob Dylan sing in my brother's bedroom before last summer started.

I stood and listened to her sing, watched her dark curls bouncing on her head as she swayed to her music.

"The answer, my friend, is blowin' in the wind, the answer is blowin' in the wind." Miss Von Schlott looked up at me, smiled at me.

I wish, I thought. *I wish the answers were blowing in the wind and I could capture them as they blew by, in my hands, like lightning bugs, or like butterflies in a net, and hold onto them or put them in a jar, twist the lid tight, and have them. Have the answers to all my questions.*

The strumming stopped. "Are you Suzanne?" Miss Von Schlott asked me.

As I nodded, she continued. "I thought so. Your brother is in Vietnam, isn't he?"

"Yes," I replied. "He used to play that song over and over. He plays the guitar, too."

I sat down next to the fourth grade teacher on the stone front porch.

"I've been warned," she told me, "that if I keep singing these songs to my class and doing other anti-war activities, as they call my expressing my opinions, that they'll fire me."

I looked at her.

"I think I can tell you that, Suzanne," Miss Von Schlott said. "I've seen you and your mother at the A&P."

"No one wants to listen," I said. "They want to pretend it's not happening, or if they talk about the war at all, they make it sound like it's great. A great adventure, not what it really is, people killing one another."

"Makes you feel pretty alone, doesn't it?" Miss Von Schlott asked me.

"I just want my brother to come home," I said.

"Me too, Suzanne, me too." Miss Von Schlott's fingers played across the strings, strumming out that Dylan tune, and I felt good sitting in the fall sunshine with this teacher who refused to be silenced. I felt not alone.

I reached down to the dirt that my sneakered feet rested on, and I drew peace signs with the tip of my finger. Over and over, a circle divided down the middle by a line, then two more lines, creating pieces of pie at the bottom. I drew peace signs in the dirt then, and on my notebooks in class, and sometimes on my hands in blue ink.

I drew peace signs over and over in the dirt, and I sang with Miss Von Schlott, our voices not rising above the noise from the playground, but together, and silenced only by the end-of-recess bell.

CHAPTER 13

Trick or Treat

Halloween, and my mother wondered about trick-or-treating, asking me, "Are you sure you're too old now, Suzanne? You always used to love trick-or-treating. I'd be glad to make a costume for you."

My mother gave up sewing when Bobby left, but she'd be willing to drag her machine from the closet, set it up, sit in front of it pushing cloth through the needle, for me. But I shook my head no, no thanks.

I used to love racing from house to house with Bobby, when my legs couldn't match his, and he'd wait for me before he'd ring the doorbell, and then together we'd run back to my father on the sidewalk, show him our loot, our full-sized Hershey bars and Tootsie Rolls, and we'd talk about what we would trade for what at the end of the evening when we would dump the contents of our bulging pillowcases out onto the kitchen table.

And then Bobby was old enough to take me himself, but too old for trick-or-treating, hanging back on the sidewalk while I navigated dark front walks and the porch steps lit only by glowing jack-o-lanterns, by myself. And instead of trading, I'd share my candy with my brother, his bounty for escorting me around the neighborhood.

And some years in between, Bobby was too old to trick-or-treat with me, not old enough yet to be my chaperone, but wanted to run with his friends, and sometimes I'd catch a flash of that year's ghoul mask as my father and I stayed on the sidewalks and Bobby and his buddies ran free through the neighborhood. One year I even cried because Bobby chose his friends over me, but my father said, "Stop, Suzanne, Bobby's growing up; he can't always have his little sister shadow trailing along

71

behind him." That night Bobby gave me one of his Hershey bars because he knew that I had cried. Maybe our mother told him. He chose his friends over me, and I tried to understand, and he tried to make it up to me.

"You're old enough to go alone, Suze," Bobby told me last October. "You don't need me anymore, and besides I have a party to go to," choosing his friends again, but of course I was older then, and I really did understand. I even thought that I could see a day coming that I might choose my friends over Bobby. Might. And so last year, I went trick-or-treating with Kathy and knew it would be my last year.

The fun leaked out of Halloween, I could have told my mother, but didn't.

"I'll stay here and hand out the candy," I said. "I know how you get tired of answering the door all night."

And since Dad's not home from work yet to help, I thought, but didn't add.

"I hope your father remembers what night it is," my mother said, "and drives carefully around all those kids."

My mother and I looked at each other, thinking the same thing, I knew. Anger doesn't help you drive. But anger is what fueled my father those days. Anger at my mother and me. Anger that he tried to keep inside, anger that slipped out not in words, but in action, driving too fast, slamming doors too hard. Anger coming between my parents, driving my mother into sleeping in Bobby's empty bed. I know because when I got up to go to the bathroom I could hear her breathing, Bobby's door slightly ajar, and I knew. One night I slipped into Bobby's room, into Bobby's bed next to my mother. She shifted over for me, sleepily made room. And even though we didn't really fit, me clinging to one edge of the bed, I stayed there with her until I heard my father's getting-up noises. Then I slipped out again, back to my own room, my own bed.

The doorbell began to ring, and I began to hand out treats, exclaiming over scary little witches and ghosts, cute and cuddly little bunnies and lambs. And then the boys in army get-ups began to arrive, jungle paint smeared on their faces, mock guns slung over their shoulders. A game to them.

And then a group of kids dressed up as hippies, mocking the hair and the clothes, and I got tired of handing out candy bars and I turned the front porch light off early, carried the candy bowl back to the kitchen.

"Aren't there any more trick-or-treaters, Suzanne?" my mother asked. "It's still early."

"No," I said. "They're done."

I set the bowl on the counter and stepped out through the sliding door, onto the concrete patio, wrapped my arms around my coatless body, glad to have shoes covering my feet, the fall chill settling in at night now. I pulled Bobby's latest letter, the one that arrived that day, out of the pocket of my jeans, unfolded it, smoothed it out, read it again, beneath the yellow glow of the back porch light.

"Hey Suzy-Q," Bobby's letter began. "Sorry I can't write as often now. We're on the move all the time and can hardly get our hands on any paper anyway. Not to mention stamps. It's getting worse here, if you can believe that. I mean, like most of the guys just want out, just want to go home like me. Makes it hard to do what we're supposed to, what we're told. Especially since what we're told to do makes no sense anymore, even makes me sick. Two guys just took off, went AWOL, said they were getting out of this war. Can they do it? Can they make it back home? I don't know, but I really want them to make it. Maybe then I could try it, but I don't know, it sounds crazy. They probably won't make it; they'll wind up dead or in jail, but I sure understand why they're trying it.

"So Suze, you guys have any plans for the holidays? Me, I'm planning on staying alive. Is Mom making turkey for

Thanksgiving? Man, it's so bad here, I'd be so happy to be home, even if it meant I had to watch Dad hack away at the turkey, complaining that the knife is too dull, or the turkey is too dry, or whatever he wants to blame it on this year.

"Don't think I'll be doing much Christmas shopping. The malls here aren't quite like they are at home. (Ha ha. That's a joke, Suze) Getting any snow yet? No, I guess not, too early for that. Hey, make sure the windows are up in the Chevy, okay Suze? I'd hate to see the snow getting in there and melting and ruining the beautiful upholstered seats.

"Ha ha. Joke. But no, kiddo, I don't remember if I closed them, so make sure for me, okay? Of course it's too late if it's been raining much, but I'd rather have the windows up, better late than never.

"Hey Suzanne, I don't think I tell you this much, or not often enough for sure, and maybe I'm just thinking this way on account of losing my buddies out here and the holidays coming, but I love you, kiddo. I know sometimes we fight and sometimes I don't want you hanging around all the time, sometimes I need my own space, space in my life for just me and maybe my friends. But I just want to make sure you know that. I really am glad you're my little sister, and when I get back I'm going to tell you that more often, Mom too, and Dad's be-a-man crap be damned. I mean it too, being in this war has taught me some stuff and when I get back I'm going to be different in some ways. But I think it's taught me different stuff than what Dad's war taught him because I know I'm way different from him and always will be. I know he thought that if I went to a war, he and I would have more in common. But he was wrong. Dead wrong. Funny, huh?

"But don't worry Suze, I'll still wake you up for midnight Monopoly marathons, and I'll still fight with Dad. Probably more now. Some things never change."

And some things do, Bobby, I thought. *If you could see Mom now, with her jeans and her hair and talking about getting a job, even arguing over and over with Dad about it and not ever jumping up to get his coffee anymore, and even me, what I care about and think about,* and I looked up into the black sky, listened to the calls of the last trick-or-treaters cutting through backyards, and I spotted a star or two. I wondered if when Bobby looked up into the sky when it was nighttime in Vietnam, if he could see the same stars. It seemed almost impossible to believe that the same sky could stretch far enough, across the entire world, to cover both of us while we slept.

CHAPTER 14

They Came While I Was At School

We didn't have turkey for Thanksgiving. But we did have snow.

I sat in the Chevy in the driveway, wiped the windshield from the inside. Wiped my breath away. I could smell Bobby in the Chevy, his sweaty after-baseball-practice mixed with chewing gum smell.

I read his last letter again. *Okay, Bobby*, I thought, *the windows are up. I made sure of that.* I folded the letter again, the creases turning gray from my hands holding it and folding it too often.

Snowflakes slid across the windshield, snowflakes landed on the hood of the engine that would never run.

They came while I was at school. I didn't have to ask my mother what they looked like, what kind of car they drove. I knew. I remembered the uniforms and dark squarish car from the day they visited the Perettis across the street.

I didn't have to ask my mother what they said. I knew. I knew when I stepped into the house, into the living room, and saw her sitting on the sofa, staring across the room, but seeing nothing.

My days were summer-plaid and popsicle-purple until Bobby had to go. My days were snow-shattered and frayed-jeaned when I knew that my brother would never come back.

The phone rang, our neighbors arrived at our door, as if on cue, with their pans, meatloaf or Jell-O salad, their words of sorrow.

My mother served slices of meatloaf, clumps of Jell-O salad, to my father and me.

"Marna," my father said, cutting into our silence like a turkey carving knife. "He had to go. Had to do his part. I'm proud of my son." My father's voice wavered, caught. I thought I could hear something besides pride in his voice. Sadness? Maybe. But he would never admit to it, I knew. It wasn't manly to be sad. And maybe he really wasn't anyway.

I stirred my Jell-O salad into mush. I didn't look up. "That's the first time you ever said that, since Bobby was a little kid," I told my father.

"Said what?" my father asked, his fork prongs stabbing into another chunk of meatloaf.

"That you were proud of Bobby," I said. "Now that he's dead, you're proud of him. Is that what it took?"

My father ignored his meatloaf, looked at me. I thought I saw wetness in his eyes. *Cry Dad*, I thought. *Just cry for Bobby*. My mother hasn't stopped crying yet. But my father wouldn't cry, I knew. Couldn't, I knew. He couldn't be sad that his son died. Only proud.

"And what good does that do now?" my mother asked from her end of the table, where she sat, shredding another paper napkin into a fluffy nest.

I took my cue, made my escape, slid onto the cold passenger's seat in the Chevy. My seat. The one I would have sat in on the way to the Tastee-Freeze.

I sat in the Chevy at night, in the driveway in the dark, away from shrieking parents, slamming doors. Sometimes my mother remembered to come out and get me, tap on the window, tell me to go to bed, sometimes she didn't. Once I slept in the Chevy all night and woke feeling the coldness all the way into my bones.

Once I dreamed about Bobby, but he wasn't in Vietnam; he was in Canada, in the Chevy, driving. I could picture him there, driving free across that wide country. I couldn't picture him in Nam; I couldn't picture the huts and swamps and secret tunnels. Maybe because I couldn't fit my brother into that picture. Maybe because I didn't want to.

I didn't know what would happen next. I didn't know what would happen if my parents could never speak to each other again without shouting. I didn't know how we'd be a family without my brother.

I didn't know how to be an only child.

But I did know that my mother and I, together, would still fight this war. Even though we couldn't bring Bobby back, we couldn't give up now. Wouldn't give up now. *My brother is gone forever*, I thought, *but I'm still here to stand up for him.*

I sat in the Chevy, and I thought about how I would grow up and probably have children. And I wondered if I would tell them that once upon a time, before they were even born, they had an uncle, and his name was Bobby, and he was my brother, and he was the best.

I sat in the Chevy and I thought about all of the questions, my mother's and my father's, from the summer and the fall, that I hadn't had the answers to. I still didn't have answers for them.

All I knew—as the snowflakes slid down the windshield and the tears slid down my cheeks—was that my brother was dead, and he would never drive his Chevy again, and I would never have the answer to my question.

Why?